"Why are you angry?

"You weren't last night. Last night you were . . . nice."

Thornton looked at her, surprised. "You were nice, too. Last night."

"Meaning that I wasn't this morning?"

"That's right. I know you're doing your job, Amanda, and I'm more grateful than I can ever tell you for getting me out of that hellhole of a prison. But I don't like being ordered about. I don't like being told what to do."

"I'm trained to do what I do. I'm a professional. I—"

"Look, we have to work together if we want to get out of here in one piece. I don't think you like me very much, and I'm not sure I like you. But for as long as we're on the island, we've got to try to get along. Agreed?"

Amanda met his gaze, her eyes serious. "Agreed."

Dear Reader,

There's so much excitement going on this month that I hardly know where to begin. First of all, you've no doubt noticed that instead of the four Silhouette Intimate Moments novels you usually see, this month there are six. That increase—an increase you'll see every month from now on—is a direct result of your enthusiasm for this line, an enthusiasm you've demonstrated by your support right where it counts: at the bookstore or by your membership in our reader service. So from me—and all our authors—to you, *thank you!* And here's to the future, a future filled with more great reading here at Silhouette Intimate Moments.

And speaking of great reading, how about this month's author lineup? Heather Graham Pozzessere, Barbara Faith, Linda Turner, Rachel Lee and Peggy Webb, making her Intimate Moments debut. And I haven't even mentioned Linda Howard yet, but she's here, too, with *Mackenzie's Mission,* one of the most-requested books of all time. For all of you who asked, for all of you who've waited as eagerly as I have, here is Joe "Breed" Mackenzie's story. This is a man to die for (though not literally, of course), to sigh for, cry for and—since he's a pilot—fly for. And he's all yours as of now, so don't let him pass you by. And in honor of our increase to six books, and because Joe and some of the other heroes I have in store for you are so special, we've decided to inaugurate a special program as part of the line: American Heroes. Every month one especially strong and sexy hero is going to be highlighted for you within the line, and believe me, you won't want to miss his story!

Finally, I hope you've noticed our bold new cover design. We think it captures the sense of excitement that has always been the hallmark of Silhouette Intimate Moments, and I hope you do, too.

In the months to come, expect only the best from us. With authors like Kathleen Eagle, Emilie Richards, Dallas Schulze and Kathleen Korbel coming your way, how can the future be anything but bright?

Leslie Wainger
Senior Editor and Editorial Coordinator

QUEEN
OF HEARTS

Barbara
Faith

Published by Silhouette Books New York

America's Publisher of Contemporary Romance

SILHOUETTE BOOKS
300 East 42nd St., New York, N.Y. 10017

QUEEN OF HEARTS

ISBN: 0-373-07446-8

First Silhouette Books printing September 1992

Printed in the U.S.A.

Books by Barbara Faith

BARBARA FAITH

is a true romantic who believes that love is a rare and precious gift. She has an endless fascination with the attraction a man and a woman from different cultures and backgrounds have for each other. She considers herself a good example of such an attraction, because she has been happily married for twenty years to an ex-matador she met when she lived in Mexico.

Prologue

Sweat ran down his back and mosquitoes buzzed around his face. But he paid them no heed, for below, there in the jungle clearing, lay the ruins of the aboriginal civilization he'd come to San Sebastian to find.

Excited, he snapped quick pictures from the camera strung around his neck, then entered the date, August 13, in his notebook, and the words, "Below me in the jungle clearing I can see what appears to be the ruins of the ancient aboriginal..." He hesitated, puzzled, and brought the binoculars up to see more clearly.

"What the devil?" he muttered.

Armed uniformed men paced up and down. To his left behind the trees he saw what he had not seen in the first excitement of discovery—wooden buildings, storage depots, something... He focused the binoculars on what to his inexperienced eye looked like a military installation and missile launchers. Missile launchers! My God! What...?

A shot rang out. He ducked, but it was too late; he'd been spotted. He turned and sprinted back the way he'd come.

He had to get to the bus, back to the group of elderly South American tourists he'd ridden out from the city with. Bird watchers. If he could get back, lose himself among them, maybe he had a chance.

He raced through the trees, knocking aside hanging branches, stumbling in his haste. His pursuers were close behind him. He heard their curses, shouted orders.

He came to the dirt road and saw a splash of color through the trees. A bright dress. Señora...what was her name? Espinoza? He called out. "Wait! *¡Espere!*"

She turned, a frightened look on her face. "Professor? What—?"

He didn't answer as he pulled the camera over his head and thrust it at her. Then, still clutching his notebook, he wrote after the notation he'd made when he first discovered the ruins, "Missile base. Prof. T. S. Thornton."

"Get this to Washington," he said.

"*No entiendo.* I don't understand," she said. "What—?"

He didn't wait to explain, but turned and raced back toward the trees. He ran almost a quarter of a mile before they caught him.

"Halt!" a voice cried out.

Bullets whistled past him. He stopped, raised his hands over his head and turned to face his captors.

They rushed at him. A rifle butt smashed against his skull. Darkness closed in around him.

Chapter 1

"I want Rebecca Bliss!"

The words, one decibel over a roar, brought everybody in the outer office to attention. Secretaries sat straighter and typed faster. Two men jumped to their feet, waiting for orders to report, but it was Ed Blakley who got up and hurried toward Hayden's office.

Alexander Hayden, head of the Washington office of Secret Intelligence Service, known in intelligence circles as SIS, thumped his desk with a beefy hand as Blakley came through the door. "Where the hell is Rebecca?" he shouted.

"Still on leave."

"She shoulda been back by now."

"She had a month. She'll be back by the end of next week."

"I want her now."

Ed Blakley eased his six-foot-six frame into the chair across from Hayden's desk. "She needs more time," he said quietly.

"I haven't got more time." Hayden shoved six black-and-white photographs and a slip of paper across his desk. "Look at these," he ordered.

Blakley raised one pale eyebrow. He read the note first, then frowned as he studied the photographs. "A missile base?" He looked at Hayden. "Where?"

"San Sebastian." Hayden got up and went to one of the many maps that covered one wall. "Here in the Caribbean," he said, pointing. "The Greater Antilles, off the southern tip of Cuba, down toward the Yucatán Peninsula."

Blakley whistled. "Within shooting distance of both Mexico and the southeast coast of the United States."

"Right. That's why I want Rebecca."

"Why Rebecca?"

Hayden motioned Ed Blakley back to his chair as he settled behind his desk. "You've heard of General Maximo Feliciano?"

"Feliciano?" Ed wrinkled his brow in concentration. "Last year... yeah, I remember now. He helped overthrow the elected president and put his own man in."

"Felipe Cardenas, puppet president. But it's Feliciano who runs things."

"What about this guy Thornton? Who is he? What do we know about him?"

"History professor. Highly respected in his field. Had a book out two years ago on the Incan civilization in Peru. I contacted the college where he teaches in Brookfield Falls, Illinois. President said Thornton had gone to San Sebastian to research a book on an ancient civilization there. He's a widower with a ten-year-old daughter. Quiet man. Pillar of the community."

"And you think he stumbled onto the missile base by accident?"

"That's the way it looks." Hayden spread his hands out flat on his desk. "If he's still alive, I've got to get him off that island, Ed. I've got to know the location of that missile site."

"You don't need Rebecca for that. Send me."

Hayden shook his head. He opened a file, took out a photograph and slid it across his desk.

Blakley studied the man in the photograph. In his late forties, Feliciano was an imposing, if not handsome figure of a man. He was smiling into the camera, but there was a coldness in his eyes, a certain firmness in the set of his jaw, a cruel sensuality to his full lips that said that this was a dangerous man. He wore a military hat; his chest was covered with row after row of medals and ribbons.

"General Maximo Feliciano," Hayden said. "Three times married, a string of mistresses. Last one, a French actress, died under mysterious circumstances. So maybe he lives up to his reputation of being a real lady killer in more ways than one."

"And Rebecca's a killer lady," Blakley said.

"That's right."

"I don't like it. Send me instead."

"She's got better legs than you have."

"Damn it, Alex—"

"She's the only one who can pull it off." Hayden ran a hand across the top of his bristly gray hair. "I know she had a tough time in Caracas, know we would have lost her if it hadn't been for you. But I need her, Ed.''

"And she needs more time to recuperate."

"I don't have more time." Hayden reached for the phone. "Where is she?"

Eyes narrowed in anger, Blakley hesitated.

"I've got to have her."

"All right, damn you, she's in Jamaica. Hotel Carlton in Ocho Rios."

A muscle jumped in Hayden's jaw. He reached for the phone.

The sun melted into her skin and seeped into her bones. She drifted with it, dazed with the heat, relishing it and the smell, the feel of sunscreen oil on her body. She loved the quiet, the peacefulness. Oh, God, yes, the peacefulness, the sense that she was safe.

She'd had the lounge taken from the crowded pool area and brought down here near the shore so that she could be alone to enjoy the turquoise-green color of the sea, the sailboats that skimmed over the surface of the water, the funny roadrunner hop-skip of the sandpipers and the cry of the gulls. She never wanted to leave here, she thought as she reached for the bottle of sunscreen. She—

"Let me do that for you."

Rebecca frowned as she squinted up at the man, automatically categorizing the carefully bronzed skin, the too-blond hair, the muscles flexed for her benefit.

"Let me do that for you," he said again.

"No, thank you."

Legs apart. Practiced smile. "Where you from?" he asked.

Rebecca picked up the novel she'd brought along just in case someone, like *this* someone, wanted to talk. "I'd really like to be alone," she said as kindly as she could.

"Aw, don't be that way. Good-looking lady like yourself should never be alone." He picked up the bottle of sunscreen, and before Rebecca could stop him he rested a beefy hand on her bare shoulder. "Umm," he murmured. "Nice. I—"

She picked up his hand and took hold of his index finger. He dropped the bottle of lotion, and his face went white beneath the bronzed tan as he dropped to his knees on the sand. "Leggo!" he yelped.

Rebecca eased up on the pressure and released him. He scrambled to his feet, cradling his finger in one hand. Muttering a string of obscenities, he took a step toward her.

"Don't," she warned in the same kindly voice she'd used before.

He hesitated. His eyes narrowed. With a curl of his lip he said, "You know, when I saw you down here all by your lonesome, I thought to myself, how come a good-looking dame like her is all alone? Well, now I know. You're tough, aren't you, sweetheart? A female barracuda. No man in his right mind would ever take more than a second look at you." He started away. "Cripes," he said. "No wonder you're alone."

Rebecca sank back on the chaise and closed her eyes. But the tears seeped under her closed lids, and she reached for her dark glasses. "Damn," she whispered. "Damn it!" And in spite of the sun that only a little while ago had seemed so warm, she felt a chill run through her body.

And knew that she really hadn't recovered from the terror that had happened to her in Caracas. She'd made a mistake, a bad one, and it had almost cost her

her life. If Ed Blakley hadn't come bursting into the terrible place where she'd been held all those weeks, she wouldn't have made it. She couldn't have held out much longer.

But Ed and the others had found her. They'd taken her to a hospital in Caracas, a place of blessed cleanliness and care, and when she was able to travel, they'd chartered a plane to take her back to the States. And, finally, when her wounds, both physical and psychological had healed, she had come here to rest and recover, and to forget.

She was better now, but she'd been badly spooked. She was more vulnerable than she'd been before or she wouldn't have let that beach-bum lothario get to her. Just because she could handle herself didn't mean she was tough or unfeminine.

Hands doubled into fists, Rebecca thumped the cushioned mat into place, then settled onto her back. "I'm not any of those things," she whispered.

But as she watched a gull float gracefully against the deep blue of the sky, the tears continued to fall.

She was dressing for dinner when the call from Washington came in.

"Rebecca?" Alex Hayden said.

"No speak the English, *señor.*"

"Cut the crap, Rebecca. I want you back here. Now."

"Sorry. I'm still on vacation. Call me in a week."

"This won't wait."

"Then get somebody else."

"There isn't anybody who can do it."

"You've got a big staff, Alex."

"Job calls for a woman."

"You've got two other women."

"Emma Stoller's almost as old as I am. Nance Sugarman is twenty pounds overweight."

"So tell her to reduce."

"This job's special. It's important."

"I've still got a week's leave."

"Leave's over. I want you in Washington tomorrow. You can pick up your ticket at the airport in Montego Bay. You get in at two-thirty. I'll have a car waiting."

"Damn it, Alex, I—" But the connection had been broken.

Rebecca put the phone down. Muttering under her breath, telling herself that Alex Hayden could go straight to hell, she headed for the closet and began to pack.

"San Sebastian?" She glared at Hayden from the other side of his desk. "I don't even know where it is."

"It's between Cuba and the Yucatán Peninsula," Ed Blakley said. "And we're pretty sure from the professor's note and from the photographs that there are missile sites there."

"If you believe what some aging wimp of a professor from Hooterville says," Rebecca said.

"Professor Thomas Thornton is a noted historian," Ed put in. "He may be from what you refer to as Hooterville, but he's one of the most respected men in his field. Here's his dossier."

She opened the manila folder. "Thomas Stanley Thornton III," she read. "Age thirty-eight. Height five-eleven. Weight one-eighty-five. Professor of history, Brookfield College, Brookfield Falls, Illinois. B.A. and M.A. University of Michigan. Ph.D. Yale."

"Egghead," she muttered. And read on. He was a widower with a ten-year-old daughter, Melinda. He had a housekeeper, a Mrs. Alvira Plum. He'd been champion of the Yale chess team, was a member of the International Historical Society, a member of the board of the Smithsonian and of the Uffizi in Florence, Italy. He belonged to Brookfield Falls Community Church and to the country club, where he played tennis once a week.

"Okay," Rebecca said. "So he's a true-blue, rah-rah all-American. He was in San Sebastian doing historical research, found the missile site by accident and got nabbed by..." She glanced at the other file on Hayden's desk. "By General Maximo Feliciano's men. If he isn't dead by now, he's rotting in one of their prison cells. What am I supposed to do? Fly into San Sebastian and single-handedly get him out?" She threw Thornton's file down onto the desk. "Get real, Alex. This is a job for either the army or the State Department. If you want my advice, it would be to send the army in."

Alex Hayden shook his head. "This is a one-woman job, Rebecca, and I'll tell you why it is." He flipped open the San Sebastian file and pointed at the photograph of Feliciano. "This is your man. General Maximo Feliciano. He's the real ruler of San Sebastian. He's strong and he's dangerous, but he's got one weak spot. He's a pushover for a beautiful woman." Hayden raised his gaze. "You're the only one I know with the looks to get close to him, close enough maybe to find out where Professor Thornton is being held."

"And when I do?" she asked, unconsciously holding her breath.

"Find out where the missile site is. Get photographs. And get Thornton." He stood up, walked over to her and put his hands on her shoulders. "I know it will be dangerous, and I wish to God I didn't have to ask it of you. But you're the best I've got and this is important, Rebecca." He tightened his hands on her shoulders. "You're the only one I know who can pull this off. I don't have a choice. It has to be you."

The thought of Melinda kept him hanging on through the beatings, the terrible isolation and the nights that were as black as death. Thoughts of the little girl who waited at home for him gave him the courage to look General Feliciano's thugs in the eye and tell them to go to hell.

He didn't know how long he'd been here. He estimated that it had been more than two weeks, but he couldn't be sure. Day after day he paced the confines of his windowless cell. Seven steps wide, eight steps long. Dirty straw mattress on one side, and a bucket that was emptied every few days. He made himself eat the food that was pushed through the floor slot: coffee and black bread for breakfast, watery soup or a gruel-like rice for dinner. He was determined to keep his strength up, determined not to lose hope.

He told himself that Señora Espinoza had sent his photographs and note on to Washington and that help would come. He had to believe that.

Next month Melinda would be eleven. He had to be home for her birthday. He promised himself he'd be home by then.

She'd been five when Beth died. Since then he'd been both mother and father, and they had managed, with the help of Mrs. Plum, to keep things going. But there were no other relatives. If anything happened to him... No, he wouldn't think about that. Help would come. It had to come. It...

He heard the footsteps, and his belly tightened with dread because he knew they were going to interrogate him again, knew they'd take him, as they did almost every day at this time to Feliciano's office.

He'd never hated anyone before, had never felt even the slightest stir of violence toward any man. But he hated the general. Hated the way the other man would lean back in his chair and smile at him. "Tell us," Feliciano would say. "Tell us you're SIS and we'll let you go."

And when, for the thousandth time, he'd say, "I'm a history professor. I don't even know what SIS is. I came to San Sebastian to do research," the general would give the order for the beatings to begin.

Thornton tightened his hands on the bars.

They unlocked his cell, and he braced himself for what lay ahead. Help had to come soon. He didn't know how much longer he could hold out.

Chapter 2

"San Sebastian, jewel of the Caribbean," Rebecca read. "Founded in the year 1513." Roughly the size of Connecticut, it boasted lofty mountains, great forests, fertile valleys, a volcano that hadn't erupted since the early seventeenth century and miles and miles of pure white sand beaches. The population was a mixture of the descendants of Carib Indians, slaves brought from Africa by the Spanish and the same Spanish who still ruled the island country.

Until a few years ago it had been one of the most traveled tourist spots in the Caribbean. Now, because of political unrest, the tourists rarely came. The cruise ships no longer stopped, and there were only two flights a week from Miami.

Which is where Rebecca had done most of her shopping.

"I want you to attract attention from the moment you step off the plane," Alex Hayden had said when he handed her three thousand dollars in cash. "I want word to filter back to Feliciano that there's a beautiful woman tourist traveling alone in San Sebastian."

Rebecca had liked the shopping part of it, the picking out and trying on of the beautifully daring swimsuits, the shorts and pants, the elegant evening wear, and the expensive white suit she'd chosen to travel in. Since she loved the islands, she told herself that as long as she had to be in San Sebastian, she might as well enjoy whatever part of it she could.

She'd read everything SIS could dredge up on General Feliciano. He'd been born on the island. He had attended school there until he was thirteen. Then he'd been sent to Spain, where he had attended a private military school in Madrid and graduated from the University of Salamanca. His parents were dead; he had no siblings.

His first two wives had been Spanish. The first wife had divorced him. The second had died in a motor accident when the brakes of the car she'd been driving failed. The third, an American, had drowned in the waters off San Sebastian. He had had numerous mistresses, both during and after his marriages. The French actress had apparently died of food poisoning.

Apparently.

Rebecca tapped silvery nails against the arm of her seat and looked out the window. In the distance she saw the green island that was San Sebastian, the latent volcano, the rise of mountains and the clean white beach that seemed to go on forever.

But as beautiful as the island was she knew that danger awaited her there because General Maximo Feliciano was a dangerous man. Would she be a match for him? Would she be able to find Professor Thornton? And if she did, would she be able to free him?

Ed Blakley had told her that ten days from today a ship would be waiting for her and Thornton just offshore on the leeward side of the island. That wasn't much time. She had to be able to find the professor and get him out of whatever prison he was in. In ten days? And when she found him would he be in any condition to travel?

Rebecca opened the new white purse, took out her makeup case and studied her face in the compact mirror as she retouched her lipstick. Her red hair was nicely coiffed and her green eyes showed no more signs of fatigue. She looked smart and expensive, a wealthy American about to spend a few weeks of fun and sun on a tropical island.

The plane circled low. She gazed down at the postage-stamp-size runway, closed her eyes and didn't open them again until the plane touched down. Then she put the wide-brimmed white hat on, gathered up her purse and makeup case and moved toward the exit with the other passengers.

Once inside the terminal she looked around, taking in every detail. There were more soldiers than passengers. Dressed in dark green uniforms, they wore holstered guns at their hips and carried Uzis. Two men with different uniforms ushered the passengers through immigration, then to the luggage carousel where customs officers waited.

"What do you have to declare, *señorita?*" a customs man asked Rebecca when her luggage was brought to him by an attendant. "Liquor? Perfume?"

"Of course." Rebecca smiled her million-dollar smile, and the customs man smiled back.

"How long do you plan to stay?" he asked.

"As long as your island pleases me," she said. "When it no longer does, I'll move on to Jamaica or perhaps Antigua."

"We have everything those islands have, *señorita*. And more. I'm sure your stay here will be a pleasant one."

"I hope so, *señor*. Am I free to go now?"

"But of course." He bowed at the waist, then signaled to a helper to take Rebecca's luggage.

As she followed the helper to the exit, she saw two well-dressed men watching her. When she passed them, one said something to the other and gave a knowing look. Feliciano's men? she wondered.

The hotel that Alex Hayden's people had chosen for her, the Royale Sebastian, was the most expensive and exclusive on the island. Her suite of rooms on the fifteenth floor overlooked the sea. They were elegantly furnished, and the balcony ran the length of both the living room and the bedroom.

She unpacked quickly and donned one of her most revealing swimsuits and a lacy jacket. "Show time," she said under her breath as she headed for the beach.

A four-piece calypso band played under the palm trees near the bar. While a beachboy fixed her lounge, she ordered a fresh fruit drink. When it came, she took off the lacy cover and stretched out, perfectly aware that she was being observed. Which was exactly why Alex Hayden had chosen her for the job. He'd wanted her to be noticed.

Rebecca sighed. Usually she simply accepted her looks, but there were times, like now, when she wasn't all that pleased that by an accident of birth she had been blessed with her mother's face and figure.

Her mother.

In the sixties Lydia Farrow had been one of the most beautiful actresses in Hollywood. Twice married and twice divorced, she'd been pushing forty when she met Rebecca's father, television producer Kevin Bliss. They had a whirlwind courtship and a honeymoon on the French Riviera. Two weeks after they returned Lydia had discovered she was pregnant, and that for her was the end of the romance. She stayed with Kevin until after Rebecca's birth, then, giving him custody, she'd taken the first plane back to California.

As a child, Rebecca's earliest recollection was of looking out the window of the high-rise New York apartment and of being taken for walks in Central Park by her father's housekeeper. She'd been almost seven when her mother visited New York to do a play and came to the apartment to see her.

For all the years after that Rebecca remembered how beautiful her mother had been, the softness of her furs and the wonderful scent of her perfume when she embraced her that first time. And she remembered the sudden shock of sadness on her mother's face. "I didn't know," her mother had said. "I'm so sorry, darling." She'd held Rebecca away from her. "I know you're too young to understand, Rebecca, but we all have choices to make and maybe..." There had been a haunting look of doubt in her beautiful green eyes. "Maybe, after all, I made the wrong choice," she had whispered.

She had seen her mother once a week for almost three months. Then the show had closed and Lydia had gone back to Hollywood.

''We'll see each other at Christmas,'' she'd said before leaving. But Christmas had come and gone and there had been no word from her.

Maybe next Christmas, Rebecca had told herself, and she'd hugged the thought to herself like a snugly warm teddy bear. But by the next Christmas Lydia had been dead, struck down by a white limousine as she was trying to cross Rodeo Drive.

''Leave it to Lydia to get hit by a limo,'' one of her father's friends had said, laughing.

And eight-year-old Rebecca had picked up a heavy glass ashtray and hurled it at him.

She hadn't liked most of her father's friends and rarely, as she had grown older, attended the cocktail parties he'd thrown for producers like himself, actors, dancers, directors, scriptwriters, costume and set designers, and the few friends from his college days at Yale who weren't in show business.

Rebecca had met Alex Hayden at one of those parties she had, at her father's behest, attended. They'd talked for a long time, not about show business, but about the state of the world, the political situation at home, the problems that had arisen with the lifting of the Iron Curtain, and the fate of the Palestinians. When the evening ended, he'd asked her to lunch and she'd accepted.

''What do you do with yourself?'' he had asked over a glass of white wine the next day.

''I'm a model,'' she said. ''And I do an occasional television commercial.''

''Like what you do?''

''Not especially.''

''Want to do something else?''

Because he wasn't the first of her father's friends to suggest an "arrangement," she narrowed her eyes in suspicion. "Like what?"

"Something that would help your country."

"Are you suggesting I join the army?" she asked incredulously.

"No," he said with a laugh. "Good heavens, no." He waited until the waiter served them. "Have you ever heard of SIS?"

"SIS?" She was honestly puzzled. "What is it? Some sort of Big Sister organization?"

"No, it's a branch of the government." His eyes were level with hers. "Like the CIA."

Rebecca stared at him. "You want me to be a spy!"

"Something like that."

"That's the most ridiculous thing I've ever heard!"

"Is it?"

"Yes! It—"

"You're a beautiful woman, Rebecca, and you're intelligent. I think you'd be a tremendous asset to our organization."

"But I—"

"Do you have any appointments this afternoon?"

"No, but—"

"Then why not let me show you around our New York office? Our main office is in Washington—that's where I spend most of my time—but our New York place has an interesting setup. There are some people there I'd like you to meet." He motioned for the waiter, impatient to leave, and signaled for the check.

Rebecca went with him out of curiosity. She met Ed Blakley and Emma Stoller and talked to a man named Eliott Donaldson, who was the head of recruiting. By the time she went home, she was in a daze. The whole thing was ridiculous. She didn't want to play cops and robbers, and she had absolutely no desire to be another Mata Hari, that infamous lady who had died in front of a firing squad.

But a month later she was in a training camp in one of the lesser known of the Florida Keys. She still wasn't sure what had made her join SIS. Perhaps it had been the need to do something different with her life, to accept a challenge to be better than she was, and to be a part of something that had some importance in the world.

That stint in the Florida Keys was the hardest two months of her life, but by the time she completed the course she felt fit and ready for anything. She learned karate, how to shoot an M-1 carbine and how to kill a man with a knife. She could assemble a rifle in a minute flat, and she could survive for a week on a quart of water and whatever game she could kill. Then there was more training in the Washington headquarters of SIS, and finally, at the end of six months, she was declared ready for duty.

She'd been twenty-five when she joined SIS; she was thirty now. It had been an exciting five years. She'd never regretted a minute of it, except for Caracas. She was good at what she did, one of the best in the business. When a job called for a woman operative, the word went out, even from other branches of the intelligence services: "Get Bliss from SIS."

She believed in what she did. Believed that bastards like this island dictator...

"I beg your pardon, *señorita?*"

Rebecca looked up at the white-jacketed bar waiter.

He held a tray with another fruit drink. "From the gentleman at the bar."

"Tell the gentleman I don't accept drinks from strangers."

"But, *señorita,* he is José Soriano, the personal assistant to General Feliciano."

"Really?" She glanced toward the bar. The man standing there was portly and middle-aged. He wore a white *guayabera* shirt, white trousers and shoes and held a Panama hat to his chest. And he was smiling in her direction.

She didn't smile back. Instead she picked up the book she was reading, along with the bottle of sunscreen and the lacy top, and went back to the hotel, completely ignoring the man at the bar.

It wasn't until she closed the door of her room that she smiled. The fish was taking the bait.

When she went down to dinner that evening, there were flowers on her table. "Compliments of General Maximo Feliciano," the waiter said.

The next morning Rebecca went down to the beach again. She had no sooner settled into her lounge chair when the portly gentleman appeared.

"Forgive me for interrupting you," he said, again with hat in hand. "I did not mean to offend you yesterday. If I did, *señorita,* I am sorry."

Rebecca didn't say anything.

"You are an American, yes?"

"Yes."

"Permit me to introduce myself. My name is José Soriano, *señorita.* I am a member of General Maximo Feliciano's staff." He cleared his throat. "This evening the general is having a dinner party for two congressmen from your country, as well as several officials from Chile and Argentina."

"I don't see how that concerns me," she said in excellent Spanish.

"Ah, you speak Spanish!" The smile broadened. "The general thought that the presence of a young American lady like yourself would add a great deal to the evening's festivities. And please allow me to assure you that everything will be quite proper. The gentlemen from Chile and Argentina will be accompanied by their wives, who I understand speak no English. And since the two American senators do not speak Spanish, you would be a most welcome, as well as a most beautiful addition to the dinner party."

"But I haven't met General Feliciano. He doesn't know me or anything about me."

Soriano smiled again. "This is a small island, *señorita*. When a woman of your obvious beauty and charm becomes a guest in our country, news travels fast."

"I see."

"You would be doing your country a great service, *señorita* if you would consent to join General Feliciano's party tonight."

Rebecca pretended to hesitate.

"Eight o'clock?" He clutched the brim of the Panama hat. "I myself will call for you."

"Very well," she said.

And the first step had been taken.

The Presidencia was a depressing gray stone building right on the *malecon,* the jettylike boardwalk that ran the length of the harbor.

Señor Soriano escorted Rebecca up the stairs where two guards stood rigidly at attention. Another guard, armed with an Uzi, said, *"Buenas noches, Señor So-*

riano. You may enter." There were two more guards inside, stationed in front of the elevator that took them to the fourth floor.

Rebecca noted everything. The Presidencia was a fortress. Impenetrable? Perhaps.

Soriano took her into a salon, shook her hand, clicked his heels and said, "Have a pleasant evening, *señorita.* I will call later to escort you back to your hotel."

A white-jacketed maître d' took her into the salon where General Maximo Feliciano waited. At first glance he didn't appear to be an imposing man. Of medium height and squarish build, his features were bland and his olive-skinned face was pockmarked. But when Rebecca looked beyond the blandness she saw that his eyes were cold and that there was a certain cruelness about the twist of his mouth. His thick black hair was slicked straight back off his wide forehead and his mustache drooped one inch from his lips. There was a military crease in the green uniform trousers, and his chest was covered with an amazing display of medals and ribbons.

"Ah, *señorita,*" he said, striding toward Rebecca the moment she entered the room. "How beautiful you look."

She had taken great pains to look her best tonight. The salon in the hotel had arranged her hair back off her face in an elegant twist, and she'd had a manicure and a pedicure. Her white beaded gown had more décolletage than she usually wore, but she had bought it for a meeting exactly like this one. Her only accessories were a pair of pearl-drop earrings and a delicate touch of perfume between her breasts. But she need not have bothered with the perfume—the overpowering scent of the general's cigar blotted out everything else in the room. It reached her before he did.

He clicked the heels of his polished boots together. "It is indeed a pleasure to meet you." He kissed her hand and, still holding it, led her to his other guests.

Mr. and Mrs. Efren Hoyos of Argentina were a pleasant-looking gray-haired couple in their late sixties. Mr. and Mrs. Ignacio Silveti of Chile were younger. He was handsome; she wasn't. The two American senators, John Harding and Louis Doyle, were both middle-aged and distinguished-looking.

Rebecca greeted the two Spanish-speaking couples in Spanish, the senators in English.

The general seated her at his right at dinner, a dinner sumptuously served by red-jacketed, white-gloved servants. Cold lobster arrived with a white French wine, chateaubriand with red...and a touch of the general's knee under the table.

Rebecca glanced at him under lowered lashes. He was speaking to the Argentinian diplomat, and though neither his voice nor his expression changed, the knee pressed insistently against hers.

Resisting the urge to bring the sharp high heel of her shoe down on his instep, Rebecca moved her leg. The general went on talking, but now it was his hand that moved under the table to rest for a brief moment on her thigh.

The conversation turned to things political, to the current government's attitude toward the United States and, as General Feliciano said with a smile to Senator Doyle, "Your country's attitude toward San Sebastian."

"We've decided on a wait-and-see policy," Senator Doyle said. "Your new president only came to power last year. To be quite frank, General, we're waiting to see what happens."

"There are several things my government questions." Senator Harding cleared his throat and looked terribly important. "We didn't approve of the methods used to remove President Aleman."

"Aleman?" With a wave of his hand Feliciano dismissed the former president. "An old man with no idea of how to run a government." He smiled. "Let me assure you, gentlemen, President Cardeñas is doing a splendid job. Since he has been in office, our crime rate has been cut in half. We plan to build more schools and hospitals in San Sebastian, more prisons." He took a sip of his wine, then stroked a drop from his mustache. "As it is, our prison system is one of the most effective in the Caribbean. We have never had an attempted escape, probably because the penalty for such an attempt is death."

"I'd like to learn more about your prison system, General." Rebecca smiled her most bewitching smile. "My father was the warden in charge of one of the largest federal prisons in the United States before his retirement."

The story had been prearranged, and if the general decided to check, sources in Washington would confirm that Kenneth, not Kevin, Bliss had indeed been a warden at one of the largest prisons in the United States.

"I grew up in a prison compound," she went on. "I've always been interested in the penal system in other countries."

"Someday I would like to discuss prison systems with your father," Feliciano said.

"My father isn't here." Rebecca looked at him over her wineglass. "But I am, General, and I have a million questions."

"Then we must certainly discuss them. Perhaps over lunch tomorrow?"

"Perhaps." She knew that both senators were shooting disapproving looks her way, but she ignored them. "Are your prisons here in the city, or do you have them farther away?"

"Our two largest are in Sabanez Province. However, we keep our most dangerous prisoners—those we are still questioning—right here in the Presidencia."

"In the Presidencia?" Rebecca chuckled. "Way down deep in the dungeons?"

"Something like that."

"I'd like to see them."

"That could be arranged."

"After lunch tomorrow?"

He leaned closer. "After lunch."

Rebecca smiled. It was done. Tomorrow she would find out where they were keeping Thomas Thornton.

They hadn't come to question him tonight. Earlier today he had heard the guards talking about a dinner party the general was giving. And one of the guards, the one called Gordo, laughed when he brought the dinner of watery soup.

"Here you are," he said. "Too bad you're not eating upstairs with the *senadores* from your country. They're having lobster and steak."

Senadores? Senators? Upstairs? Hands clutching the bars, Thornton asked, "From the United States? Are you sure?"

"Of course I'm sure, *cabrón*. My brother works in the kitchen. There are big shots from Argentina and Chile, as well as the *senadores*."

Gordo shoved the soup through the slot at the bottom of the cell. "Too bad you weren't invited, but then you're not dressed for it, are you? And you're dirty, Mr. American. So dirty you smell."

"Then, damn it all, bring me some water so I can bathe."

Gordo shook his head. "I can't do that, *señor*. The general wants you as you are—bruises, cuts, beard and dirt. He thinks it makes a man humble."

"How long are they going to keep me here?"

"*¿Quien sabe?* Who knows?" Gordo shrugged. "Until you tell them what you know."

"But I don't know anything! I've told them that. I—"

But Gordo turned away, and he was alone again.

Day after day they had accused him of being an SIS agent. And day after day he had told them he had come to San Sebastian for the sole purpose of finding whatever traces were left of the ancient aboriginal civilization that had once lived on the island. He was a scholar, he'd said. A historian.

Early on, before the beatings had become so bad, he'd added with a trace of humor, "Look here, fellows, do I look like a James Bond type?"

They hadn't been amused.

He had never lost hope that he would be rescued. Now there was hope. His message and the film had gotten to Washington. That was why the senators were here. They were trying to free him by diplomatic means. That had to be it. It had to be.

Thornton made himself drink the watery soup. Then he lay down on the dirty straw mattress. Tomorrow, he thought. Perhaps by tomorrow he would be free.

All through that long dark night he clung to the thought of freedom.

Chapter 3

From the moment they entered the restaurant the general behaved like a strutting peacock, all but twirling his waxed mustache whenever he looked at Rebecca. He touched her every chance he had, small pats on her hand, her shoulder, her thigh. The food, though good, stuck in her throat. She wanted to dump her vichyssoise onto his lap and get the hell away from him. But she didn't. Instead she made herself smile and say all of the right things.

He talked about himself and his many accomplishments, about his days in Spain, the military school, and the University of Salamanca.

"I'm the youngest general in the Caribbean," he told her with pride. "I'm the one who runs San Sebastian, not the president. Even the president does what I say."

Rebecca encouraged him with wide-eyed admiration, a flirtatious lowering of her lashes and a gentle smile whenever she moved his hand from her thigh and admonished, "Now, General, behave yourself."

And she made herself say yes when he asked her, in a sexily suggestive voice, if she would have dinner with him the following evening in his suite at the Presidencia. "Will there be other guests?" she asked.

He stroked her cheek. "Of course not."

"Then I'd be delighted to come."

He laughed and kissed her fingertips. "You're a delicious woman. I can barely wait for tomorrow night."

Nor can I, Rebecca thought. Then she said, "Remember, General, you promised that today you would show me those deep, dark dungeons you have hidden down in the bowels of the building."

"Not actually dungeons, my dear, but close enough. If you really are interested—"

"I'm interested."

"Very well. I'll take you on a personally conducted tour." He signaled for the check.

A tour of the prison. Rebecca's heart quickened. She was going to find out where the professor was being held. That was the first step in getting him out.

Thornton had spent an almost sleepless night. The news that two American senators were here in San Sebastian had given him new hope. Perhaps even now the discussions were taking place. Someone would come for him. He'd be released. There would be an official apology.

The first thing he would do would be to ask for a telephone and call Melinda. He wondered what they'd told her. She was a brave little kid, but he had a pretty good idea how she'd take it if they'd told her her dad was locked up in some island prison. Mrs. Plum was a good woman. She'd stay on at the house for as long as she was needed, but she had her own family, her own concerns. If something happened to him, the state would step in. Melinda would be put in a foster home. She . . .

No, he wouldn't think about that. It was going to be all right. Washington had sent two representatives of the American government to expedite his release. It was only a matter of time.

Gordo brought his too-weak coffee and black bread a little after nine. He wolfed it down, so hungry he felt like his stomach was touching his backbone. He promised himself that the second thing he was going to do was have a decent meal. And real coffee. God, what he wouldn't give for a good strong cup of coffee.

After he ate, he did the exercises he'd made himself do every day since his capture—push-ups, leg lifts, squats, everything he could think of to strengthen his muscles, to give some semblance of keeping in shape. And all the while he did them he thought, Maybe today. Maybe today I'll be free.

It was after two that Thornton heard the sound of footsteps and a woman's laughter, laughter like the sound of spring rain. He ran to the bars, and the breath caught in his throat because she was so beautiful, so fresh and so clean. Her hair, a luxurious red, was soft around her face. She wore a pink dress with a short skirt that showed off her long legs, and high heels that tapped on the cold concrete floor. He caught the scent of her perfume when she came closer.

"This is truly the most dreadful place I've ever seen." She shuddered delicately and clung to the general's arm. "All of the men are so dirty, so..."

She spoke English!

"I'm an American!" he called out. "My name is Tom Thornton. Tell the senators. Tell them I'm here!"

She looked at him, up and down with cool green eyes. "He's so *dirty,*" she said to the general. "Don't you ever let your prisoners bathe?"

"Not this one."

The delicate patrician nose wrinkled in disdain.

"Damn it!" he yelled. "I need help. Tell—"

"Guard!" Feliciano shouted, and the one called Manuel ran forward.

"*Sí,* my general?"

"I want that man silenced. At once!"

"Wait!" Thornton called out. "Wait! I—"

The rifle butt smashed against his head. He staggered back and fell to the dirt floor.

"You do have a way with your prisoners," he heard the woman say. And she laughed again, that same springtime laugh.

"Bitch," he whispered just before the darkness came. "Bitch..."

Rebecca stood in the shower for a long time. She scrubbed her skin again and again as though by sheer force of will she could wash away the stench of the place where she had been, the memory of those dirty unshaven men. Of Thornton and the look on his face when he cried out to her for help.

The sound of her own laughter echoed in her ears, and of his whispered words, "Bitch. Bitch."

She'd seen the bruises on his arms and face, the dried blood. She'd heard the whomp of the rifle butt against his skull.

She swore under her breath and called the general every name in her seldom-used vocabulary of obscenities.

"Hold on, Thornton," she said aloud. "Hold on. I'm coming."

She was admitted to the general's suite by a servant in a gray uniform. Feliciano came immediately to greet her. He kissed both her cheeks, and to the servant he said, "That will be all for tonight, Gustavo. You may go now." He put his arm around Rebecca's waist. "I've let all the servants off, my dear. I hope you don't mind, but I thought we might enjoy being alone. My chef has prepared a splendid cold dinner for us, which we shall have whenever we're ready. Now come, tell me what you think of my quarters."

They were all glass and chrome, and a clash of colors that set Rebecca's teeth on edge, as did the red velvet smoking jacket with ribbons and medals strewn across his chest. Did he wear them to bed? she wondered, and the thought sent a shiver down her spine.

She sipped the champagne he poured before he settled onto the bright blue sofa next to her, and told herself, even as she smiled at him, that this would be over soon. Tonight she would rescue Thornton and, God willing, she'd never have to see Feliciano again.

Today she had rented a Jeep from the hotel, and as soon as it was dark, she'd driven it to the stand of trees close to the Presidencia. The things she and Thornton would need were locked inside. Yesterday, when they left the cells, she had found out from Feliciano that only one guard was on duty at night. She could handle that. Her biggest worry was whether or not Thornton would be able to walk to the Jeep.

"You look lovely tonight."

"I . . . I beg your pardon."

"Ah, your thoughts were elsewhere. I must do something about that, yes?" He slid his arm from the back of the sofa onto her shoulder. "You really are the most amazingly beautiful woman I've ever seen, *mi querida* Rebecca." He took an hors d'oeuvre from the tray in front of them and held it to her lips.

She nibbled at it and steeled herself not to draw away when he ran his fingers across her lips.

"I've seen you in white and in pink. Tonight you're wearing black. I think I like that best of all."

Yes, black, Rebecca thought, so that I can disappear into the shadows once I take care of you, my general.

She'd chosen the black silk jumpsuit and the ballet-type slippers carefully. The outfit, while tight-fitting and sexy, allowed her great freedom of movement. It would help her in her attempt to free Thornton tonight.

Feliciano leaned back against the cushions and urged her closer. "My beautiful American," he said, kissing her.

His lips were wet and spongy-soft against hers, and only by the sheer force of her will did Rebecca make herself relax against him. "Nice," she said when she broke away. "But I have bad news, Maximo." She smiled her most charming smile. "May I call you Maximo?"

"Of course, *querida*." He made as though to bring her down beside him again. "But what is your bad news."

"I'm thirsty." She glanced at the almost-empty champagne bottle. "There's barely enough for one glass. Could we have a little bit more before dinner?"

"You may have anything you want, lovely lady. I myself will get it for you if you promise not to move."

"I promise, Maximo." She patted the place next to her on the sofa and leaned back. "Hurry," she whispered. "I'll be waiting."

She waited until she heard the click of the door, then quickly opened her evening purse and took out a small perfume vial. Next to it there was a cigarette lighter type of gadget and a gun. But they were for later. She opened the vial and spilled the contents into the general's glass, then poured the rest of the champagne into his glass.

When he came, she handed him his champagne. He filled her glass and said, "*¡Salud!*" before he settled in beside her, one arm around her shoulders. "I learned about champagne from my third wife. She was French."

"Oh?"

"A lovely creature really, but with an absolutely vile temper."

She knew, but because she thought she should evidence interest, she asked, "What happened to her?"

"She died, poor thing." He took a sip of his champagne.

"That's too bad."

"Yes, isn't it." He drained his glass. "Are you terribly hungry?" he asked, nuzzling her ear.

"Not terribly."

He chuckled, then yawned. "Sorry. Maybe I've had too much champagne. Perhaps we should eat."

Rebecca settled back onto the sofa and looked up at him. "Whatever you want," she murmured.

"You know what I want. I..." He yawned again.

"Why don't you snuggle down next to me for a couple of minutes?" She drew him closer. "That's it, Maximo. That's it."

"I don't know what...sleepy. Can't seem to focus. Something's wrong...something in my drink... You put...put something in my..." He fought to stay awake. "You..."

He slumped against her, and she eased him down against the pillows. When she got up, she dimmed the lights. Then she picked up her evening bag, went to the door and opened it. There was no one in the corridor when she slipped out and closed the door. Ignoring the elevator, she headed for the enclosed stairway that would take her down the seven flights to the cells below.

As she descended, she said a small, fervent prayer that everything would go the way she had planned.

He couldn't sleep. He paced up and down the narrow cell. His head thrummed with pain, but nervous energy and an anger unlike anything he'd ever known kept him on his feet. Anger at the guard who had struck him yesterday, and that strutting General Feliciano with his Napoleonic complex and pockmarked face. But most of all his anger was directed at the woman who had laughed at him. She was a fellow American. She had seen his plight and she had laughed. He would never forget that, or her.

He had heard the guards talking about the general's penchant for women. "He beds them, keeps them as long as it suits him, then discards them," they'd said. And the skinny one called Jacinto had whispered to Manuel, "It's said that if they don't go willingly, he assists them...." The guard looked around to make sure no other ears except Manuel's, and of course, the prisoner who didn't count heard. "He assists them out of this world," he'd finished.

Thornton would like to assist *her* out of this world. Like to get his hands around that slender white neck. Like to... He paused. He heard something. A footstep?

He looked at Manuel, who sat slumped in a straight-backed chair, asleep, the rifle leaning against the wall beside him. The guard didn't stir. But there was something. Something...

There, in the shadows, he saw the figure in black. Oh, God, he thought, they'd come for him again. His stomach clenched and his hands tightened on the bars until his knuckles went white. Then he saw the red hair. The woman! My God, it was the woman!

He opened his mouth to speak, but before he could she held a cautioning finger to her lips and started toward Manuel. The guard stirred and opened his eyes. Before he could cry out she sprayed something in his face. He covered his eyes with his hands, and when he did, she jabbed a needle into his arm, clapped a hand over his mouth and held him until he slumped to the floor. Quickly she began going through his pockets. When she found the keys, she ran to Thornton's cell. The first key didn't fit. She swore under her breath and tried another one. It fitted, and the door swung open.

He stared at her. "Who are you? What are you—?"

"Don't stand there like an idiot. Help me get him undressed."

She ran back to Manuel, pulled his shoes off and began tugging at his trousers. "Come *on!*" she whispered. "Get his shirt off."

He did what she said, not understanding, wondering who she was and why she was here. And whether or not this was some kind of a trap.

They got the clothes off Manuel. He pulled his own clothes off and put the uniform on. He'd lost weight and had to cinch Manuel's belt tight to keep the pants up.

"This way," the woman said, impatient to leave.

They started into the corridor she'd emerged from. He followed her until they came to the stairway, went one flight up and stopped in front of a door.

"Wait here," she said.

Thornton waited.

She took a look outside, then came back to him. "I've got a Jeep parked over in the trees about thirty yards from here." In the dim light she looked him up and down. "Are you strong enough to make it?"

"I can make it."

She nodded. "Stay close to me."

I wouldn't have it any other way, Thornton thought. At least not until I know what this is all about.

They edged along the side of the building for maybe nine or ten feet. "Here we go," she whispered. "Keep low and keep quiet."

He felt as if he ought to salute, but didn't.

They moved toward the trees. Halfway there they heard a sound. She turned quickly, and with a hand against the middle of his back, shoved him facedown onto the grass. He waited, scarcely breathing. There was no other sound. He had to resist the urge to get up and run for the trees. Now that he was out of the hated cell, all he could think about was putting some distance between himself and it.

Five minutes passed before she gave him the signal to get up. She sprinted toward the trees; he lumbered. His wind was gone. Three weeks of near starvation had weakened him.

By the time he reached the Jeep, she'd unlocked her door and had reached in to unlock his side. He slid into the seat and she started the engine. "You okay?" she asked.

"Okay," he managed to say.

She backed the Jeep out from under the trees.

"Where are we going?"

She shot him a grin. "Away from here."

"Who are you?"

"Name's Bliss. I work for SIS."

"Bliss from SIS? Yeah, sure." He looked at her, not believing anything she'd said. "And they sent you to get me out?"

"Strange as it seems, yes."

"I thought maybe the senators—"

Rebecca shook her head. "I doubt they know anything about you." She spun the car onto the road that led out of town. "I had ten days to get you out and meet the boat that's going to be waiting for us. I did it in four. That leaves us six days to kill."

"Six days!" Any minute now somebody would discover he was missing and a search party would come looking for him. San Sebastian was a small island; the soldiers would spread out. He and the woman wouldn't be that difficult to find.

''What in hell are we supposed to do for six days?''
he asked.

''Find a place to hole up.'' She frowned. ''What did
you want me to do, Thornton? Let you stay in the cell
until they finished you off?''

His lips tightened. ''What about the general?''

''I took care of him.''

''How?''

''Old-fashioned mickey. He'll sleep like a baby for
the rest of the night.''

''How did you manage that?''

''A couple of drops in his champagne. In his...uh,
in his quarters.''

''Oh.''

''It was the only way I knew to get you out,'' she
said.

She had rescued him and he was grateful to her for
that. But he didn't like her. It was that first image of
her that had seared into his brain, the imperious way
she'd looked at him, that mocking laugh. Or maybe it
was the way she had of giving orders. It wasn't a man-
woman thing, the fact that she was in charge. He'd
worked with women for years, women he'd liked and
respected. But he didn't like this woman.

They were on the beach road now and he could
smell the sea, salt-fresh and tangy. Escape lay somewhere out there at sea. Six days from now. But where
were they going to hide until then?

Chapter 4

They'd gone almost five miles when Rebecca pulled the Jeep over to the side of the road. "Change places with me," she said. "It looks like there's a checkpoint up ahead. You're wearing a uniform. It's better that you drive."

But when he started to get out and come around, she said, giving orders again, "No, you slide over. I'll come around."

And when he did, and she slid into the seat beside him, she asked, "How's your Spanish?"

"I get by."

"I hope so."

Thornton tightened his hands on the steering wheel and started the car. A quarter of a mile ahead they came to the checkpoint. "There it is," he murmured under his breath. As they drew closer he stopped and lowered the window of the Jeep. *"Buenas noches. ¿Que tal?* How goes it?"

"Quiet night, *Sargento.*" The guard looked in through the window and grinned. "I see it goes well with you."

Thornton forced a laugh. "Better than you think, *compañero.*" He started the Jeep, and with a wave of his hand moved slowly so as to avoid suspicion.

"You handled that well," Rebecca said. "Now pull over and let me drive."

"Why? Have you ever been down this road before? Do you know where you're going any better than I do?"

"I've studied the maps."

"Then you be the navigator. I'll drive. I usually do when I'm with a woman." He frowned. "Besides, you drive too fast."

Rebecca's teeth clenched. "I'm an expert driver. And I'm in charge. I—"

"Have you got anything to eat?"

"You're hungry?"

"No lady, I'm not hungry. I've been fed two sumptuous meals a day for the past couple of weeks—weak coffee and stale bread in the morning, watery soup at night. No reason to be hungry."

Frowning, Rebecca reached into the back seat. When she found an apple, she handed it to him. "Maybe this will help."

He ate two apples and half a box of crackers before he said, "That'll hold me for now." Then he settled back with both hands on the wheel. "Do you have any idea where we're heading?"

"Our rendezvous is way down on the north shore, beyond a place called Grenville. Six days from now. It was a hangout for the buccaneers in the old days. Henry Morgan used to headquarter there."

The six days worried him. By tomorrow morning, when Gordo came to replace Manuel, the word of his escape would be out. Maybe even sooner, depending on the strength of the mickey the woman had given Feliciano. Once the general came to he'd know she'd given it to him, and he'd be after both of them. "Can't you communicate with whoever it was who sent you here to pick us up before the appointed date?" he asked.

"I'm going to try," she said. "Tomorrow. There's a place not too far from here where I thought we might spend the night. Plantation House. It's listed in the travel brochure on the island. From what information I could gather it's off the main road, right on the sea. I think we'll be all right there, at least for the night."

"I can't go into a hotel looking like this."

Rebecca looked at him. "No, I don't suppose you can." She pointed to a place ahead, just off the road. "Pull over and stop." When he did, she swiveled and began to rummage through the things on the back seat. Finally she handed him a bar of soap. "Go take a bath in the sea. I'm sorry I forgot to buy any towels, but the air will dry you off."

"And what am I supposed to put on once I'm clean?"

"Clean clothes. They're in the back, too. I'll get them while you bathe."

Too tired to argue, Thornton took the soap and headed across the road. He stripped out of the green uniform and, wearing only his briefs, waded into the water. Clutching the soap in one hand, he started into deeper water. The salt water stung, even as it cleansed the cuts and bruises. He swam until he began to tire and until his breath became ragged. Finally, waist-deep, he discarded the briefs and began to wash. When he was rinsed off, he looked toward shore. The woman was standing there, waiting.

His briefs had gone out with the tide; he was naked. Now what was he supposed to do? He started wading in.

"I...I'll just leave the clothes here," she called out, then turned and hurried toward the car.

Her face burned, and all she could think of was that Professor Thomas Stanley Thornton III didn't look like a wimp. He was all man, from the top of his slick wet hair all the way down to his muscular legs. And everything in between. That unsettled her.

From the refuge of the Jeep she darted a look at him. She'd told him before he went into the water that he'd have to dry out in the air, and that was what he was doing, standing there naked, feet apart, looking out toward the sea.

Rebecca looked away, eyes straight ahead, and kept them that way until he came back to the Jeep, wearing one of the pairs of khaki shorts she'd bought, a T-shirt and sandals.

"Better?" he asked.

She nodded. "You'll do." And, having confiscated the driver's seat once more, she started the car.

Fifteen minutes later they saw the sign that read: Plantation House. Guest Rooms and Cottages.

"This is it," she said, slowing the car. "We'll use my boss's name, Hayden, Alexander Hayden."

"Mr. and Mrs.?"

Rebecca's mouth tightened. "It's better that way. We don't want to do anything to arouse suspicion."

"Whatever you say, lady."

"My name is Rebecca."

"But never Becky."

"Never."

"That's what I thought."

She shot him a look, then slowed and stopped the Jeep in front of the sign that read Office. Thornton got out, and knowing better than to go around and open her door, waited until she got out. They went into the office together. The woman behind the desk looked up when they came in.

"I know it's terribly late," Rebecca said, "but—"

"We have a reservation," Thornton cut in. "Mr. and Mrs. Hayden from New Jersey. My wife had our travel agent there make the reservations over a month ago."

"I don't recall the name," the woman said.

"Please check." Thornton's voice was firm, authoritative.

She did, then said, "I'm sorry, sir. I can't seem to find it."

"You *did* make them, didn't you?" he asked Rebecca.

"Well, I—"

"I knew I should have done it myself." Exasperated, he turned back to the woman behind the desk. "Surely you have something for us."

"Yes, of course. I have a nice one-bedroom cottage right on the water. I'm sure you'll like it, Mr. Hayden." She turned the registration slip toward him, and he registered as Mr. and Mrs. Alexander Hayden, 223 Harbor Drive, Camden, New Jersey.

"How long will you be staying?" she asked.

"Three or four days," he said. "Perhaps longer."

She handed him a key. "I'll have someone get your bags."

"That isn't necessary," Thornton said, because he didn't know whether or not they had any bags. "Just direct me. I'll take care of the things." He took Rebecca's arm. "Come along, dear. I know how tired you must be."

She didn't speak until they were outside. Then she yanked her arm away. She didn't like his taking over. She was in charge of this operation and she expected him to take orders from her, not the other way around. As soon as they were settled in, she planned to make that abundantly clear.

But by the time they had brought the things in from the Jeep, it was evident that Thornton had had about as much as he could take. By the overhead light in the living room, she saw more clearly than she had before how haggard his face was, and the dark patches of fatigue beneath his eyes.

"You take the bedroom," she said. "I'll sleep out here."

"But—"

"No argument, Professor. You aren't going to be able to make it if you don't get some rest."

He ran a hand across his whiskery face, too tired to argue. "You'll be okay out here on the couch?"

"Of course." Rebecca handed him one of the backpacks she'd bought the day before. "You'll find a razor and other clothes inside. Sorry, I didn't think to buy pajamas."

"I never wear them."

"Oh." She cleared her throat. "Well, then...I'll see you in the morning, Professor Thornton."

"Thomas. Or Tom, whichever you prefer."

"But never Tommy," she said, getting back at him for the Becky thing.

"Never." He managed a tired smile, then went into the bedroom and closed the door.

He could smell bacon frying, and lay with his eyes closed, still in that half stage between waking and sleeping. Mrs. Plum was in the kitchen, Melinda would be getting ready for school. All was right with his world.

A pan thumped. He opened his eyes and knew that, after all, he wasn't at home, but here on the island of San Sebastian with a woman by the name of Bliss who had rescued him and brought him here. He was free and he was safe, at least for the moment. And this was the first good night's sleep he'd had in a long time.

He stretched and groaned as he headed for the bathroom. Every bone and muscle in his body hurt. He got into the shower and stayed under the hot water for a long time. When he finally came out, he dried himself. Then, with the same towel, he wiped off the mirror and took a good look at himself.

He looked like hell—face drawn, body thinner and covered with bruises. "Bastards," he said under his breath, and reached for the razor.

After he shaved, he put on the same pair of khaki shorts he'd worn the night before, and though it was hot in the cottage, he pulled one of the T-shirts over his head because he didn't want Bliss to see the bruises.

Rebecca, never-Becky, Bliss. What kind of woman was she? he wondered. Competent, he decided. And professional. She'd taken care of the guard and she'd gotten him out of that hellhole of a prison. As much as she irritated him, for all that he didn't like her, he had to hand it to her. She knew what she was doing.

"Here you are," she said when he went out into the living room. "You look better. Did you sleep well?"

"Yes." He took the glass of orange juice she handed him and nodded his thanks. "And you?"

"Fine." She turned her attention back to the stove. "A maid came in this morning to fix breakfast, but I told her just to leave everything, that I'd do the cooking. I thought it best she didn't see you in case a description is already out."

"Did she seem suspicious at all?"

"No, I don't think so. She was very nice. Her name is Hortensia, and she kept admiring my I Love Paris T-shirt so I gave it to her. She was too excited about that to be suspicious."

Rebecca poured the eggs she'd been mixing into a frying pan. "I've set the table outside on the terrace. I figured you could use some sun. After we eat, I'd like to check you over."

He raised one eyebrow. "Why?"

"To make sure you're all right. I brought a first-aid kit along."

"I'm all right," Thornton said.

"You've had a difficult time. I know you were mistreated. I saw them hit you."

"And you laughed." His eyes narrowed. "I heard you. No maidenly distress when the guard clubbed me, no girlish scream, just a laugh."

Her hands hovered over the stove. "I had to make the general think it didn't matter," she said in a voice so low he could barely hear her.

"You were pretty convincing, lady." He turned, stalked out onto the terrace and stared at the sea. He tried to still the anger that had flared, to tell himself she'd only been doing her job. But the sound of her laughter still rang in his ears.

She came out, carrying two plates heaped with bacon and scrambled eggs. He sat down. She went back into the kitchen and returned with a basket of warm croissants and a dish of sliced mangoes.

"First real food I've had in almost three weeks," he said, breaking the silence.

"Was it bad?" she asked. "Being locked up?"

"It wasn't good."

"Tell me about it, about how they captured you, I mean. I'll need to know the exact location of the missile site so I can mark the location and take photographs."

"I thought we were headed toward a rendezvous with your boss."

"We are. But first I have to know where the missiles are."

"And I'm going to take you to them."

"That's right."

"So this wasn't just a rescue mission." He poured coffee into her cup, then his. "Not just a philanthropic gesture on either your part or your organization's." He looked across the table at her. "You got me out because I know where the missile site is."

"That was part of it." She met his gaze. "But not all. You're an American citizen. We—"

He raised his hand, stopping her. "Spare me."

"You *do* know where it is?"

"Yes."

"Where?"

"Inland. Near the volcano. Near a town..." He wrinkled his brow in concentration. "Villa Nova.

That's where the bus left us off, the South Americans and me. If we can get to Villa Nova, I'll know where we are.''

"We'll rest another night," Rebecca said with a nod. "I asked the maid if they had a fax machine or a telephone. They haven't got either one, so I can't send a message. Sorry. First thing in the morning we'd better head for Villa Nova." She stood up and began to clear the dishes.

"I'm going to take a walk on the beach." Without thinking he pulled the T-shirt over his head.

Rebecca saw the bruises, the scabbed-over cuts, the burns. And gasped.

"Compliments of your General Feliciano," Thornton said in a hard voice. He saw her recoil, and there was a part of him that knew he was being unreasonable, that she'd had to cozy up to Feliciano in order to get him out. To make up for it he said, "I haven't thanked you for rescuing me. Thank you." Before she could answer he turned and strode down toward the water.

He came back an hour later, carrying the khaki shorts. He'd been swimming. Droplets of water clung to his body. The low-slung black briefs she'd bought for him were wet and clinging, leaving absolutely no doubt of his incredible masculinity. Rebecca looked at him, then away as something unbidden stirred in the lower regions of her body. This was the second time she'd seen him naked or almost naked; it had to stop.

They were having dinner that night when the same maid who had brought their breakfast, a small, dark-skinned woman in her mid-thirties, knocked and walked in. "I came to see if there was anything I could do, *señora*," she said.

"No, thank you, but perhaps if you came back in a little while you could clear up the dishes."

"Yes, of course." She smiled shyly at Thornton, then hesitated, her brow wrinkling with a frown. She seemed about to speak, but didn't.

"What is it?" Rebecca looked at Thornton, then back at the woman. "Is something wrong?"

The woman began to edge toward the door. "No, *señora*. I...I have other rooms to attend to. I..." She took a steadying breath, looked at Rebecca, hesitated, then said quickly, as though to do it before she changed her mind, "There was news on the radio this afternoon about an escaped prisoner. An American." She darted another look at Thornton. "It said that soldiers are checking all of the hotels along the coast and that roadblocks have been set up."

"I see." Rebecca wet her lips. "Well, that . . . that's very interesting."

The maid started toward the door. "I will return later to clean the kitchen."

"Perhaps in thirty minutes."

"Very well, *señora*. Thirty minutes."

Rebecca stood and offered her hand. "Thank you, Hortensia."

"Por nada, señora." With a bob of her head the maid hurried out.

"She knew the minute she looked at me," Thornton said when the woman was gone.

"Yes." Rebecca started toward the living room. "We've got to leave."

He was two steps behind her, heading toward the bedroom where he gathered up the things he'd used the night before. His heart pounded. He knew he was afraid of going back, afraid of the beatings. And knew, too, that he would do anything he had to do not to be taken again.

When he came out into the other room, he saw that Rebecca was ready, and that she'd left money on the sink for the maid. "All set?" she asked. Her voice was steady and calm.

"All set," he said, and they hurried out to the Jeep.

Rebecca got into the driver's seat. He didn't argue.

"No radio?" he asked. She shook her head.

"We'll head inland toward the mountains. Away from the roadblocks."

But they had to find the inland road first, had to keep to the coast road until they did. They drove without lights, guided by a quarter slice of new moon. Thornton leaned forward in his seat, trying to see through the darkness.

"We've got to find a road soon," Rebecca said under her breath. "It has to be along here somewhere. The map—"

"Stop!" He clamped a hand on her thigh. "There's a roadblock up ahead."

She cut the engine. Ahead of her through the darkness she could see the guards, lights and the sawhorses blocking the road. She looked to the right, to a place where she could pull off. But the trees were thick here; there was nowhere to go.

"Head for the beach," Thornton said.

She started the Jeep, engine purring low, and prayed they wouldn't get stuck. They had no choice. They had to go back. They—

A shout rang out. A searchlight flashed on the road where they had been. Rebecca gunned the engine and turned the Jeep toward the beach. She felt the sand grab the tires and prayed again that they wouldn't get stuck.

Behind them they heard a siren. Thornton swung around and saw the glow of headlights a hundred or so yards back on the road. "Keep going," he said. "Don't stop."

"The sand—"

"It'll be easier going near the shore. Try to—"

The Jeep sloughed to the right and stopped. Rebecca stomped hard on the accelerator; the tires spun and sank deeper into the sand.

"It's no use," she cried. "We're stuck."

He reached into the back and grabbed both packs. "Let's go!" he shouted over the whine of the siren. "Toward the water. Come on."

They sprinted toward the shoreline. Halfway there, she saw the rocks blocking their way and hesitated, not sure which way to go.

"We'll go over or around them." Thornton grabbed her hand and raced with her toward the rocks. They extended too far into the sea for them to go around, so instead of trying they climbed over those nearer to the shore, clawing for a handhold, a foothold. The moon had disappeared behind the clouds; it was difficult to see. He went ahead of her and pulled her up after him. Then they were over, back on the sand, running.

A shot rang out. She heard voices crying out, "*¡Adelante!* Forward. We've got to find them!"

Thornton saw an overhang of trees, more rocks, darkness. The moon came out from behind the clouds, and he saw what looked like the entrance to a sea cave. He gripped Rebecca's hand and headed toward it.

"Get inside," he said.

"No. No, I—"

He pushed her in ahead of him. She stumbled and fell. The sand was damp. She heard him behind her, pulling branches over the entrance, backing in, covering their tracks.

"Listen," she said, scrambling to her feet. "I can't—"

"Shh!" He shoved her back down against the damp sand and lay beside her. The voices came closer. He saw the flash of a light.

"They came this way," a voice said.

"Search down toward the beach," another man said. "They may have started swimming."

"Or gone back the other way." There was a shouted command, then the order, "Spread out. We have to find them."

The voices receded.

Rebecca got to her hands and knees. "They've gone," she whispered. "Let's get out of here."

But Thornton shook his head. "They may have left a man or two to watch this section of the beach. We can't leave. Not yet." He stood, and because the ceiling of the cave was so low, he had to bend his head. "Let's go farther back where there's more room."

She started to say, No, I can't do that. I really can't do that. But she didn't let herself say the words. She had to remember that she was in charge, that Thornton was her responsibility. She couldn't, she wouldn't let her fear overwhelm her.

She would not.

Chapter 5

Darkness choked her, the dampness chilled. She could smell the sharp salt sting of the sea and feel it creeping closer.

"The tide's coming in," Thornton said. "We've got to move farther back."

"I'd rather stay here near the entrance."

"But the water's rising," he said in a reasonable voice. "We can't go outside because of the soldiers. We haven't any choice. We have to go farther into the cave." He slung his backpack off, reached inside for the flashlight he'd seen there yesterday and started forward. Rebecca didn't move. Seawater swirled around her ankles, but she stayed where she was.

When he saw she wasn't following him, he said, "We don't have any choice. We have to go farther back." He shone the light on her face. Her eyes were wide with fear; she was poised as though for flight, ready to bolt and run. And suddenly Thornton knew he had to stop her before she did. He had to do something to shock her out of her fear.

He gave a bitter, dry laugh, and in a deliberately harsh voice he said, "So this is what the government has sent to rescue me. A woman who's afraid of her own shadow! Bliss from SIS! You're a real winner, lady. If you're the best they've got, we're in big trouble."

"You don't understand." She wet her lips. "I—"

"Stay here if you want to," he said scornfully, and turned his back on her.

"Wait," she whispered. "You...you don't understand." She hesitated, torn between escape and the knowledge that he was right. The water was rising. They couldn't stay where they were.

"Come on," he said again, and she took a deep breath and followed him.

The floor of the cave rose. Except for the pinpoint glow of the flashlight they were in total darkness. Rebecca wanted to beg him to stop, and clamped her teeth hard on her lower lip so that she wouldn't.

At last he stopped and said, "We can wait here." He put the backpack down. "It's going to be a long night. We might as well try to rest."

Rebecca sat beside him, teeth chattering, hands clenched together. She tried to blot out the sound of the encroaching sea. And the memory of Caracas, of that small place near the island of Margarita where she had been held in the darkness of a cave like this one.

She began to shake. Thornton felt it and asked, "What is it? Are you afraid of caves?"

"Yes, I...I guess so. I always have been, but it wasn't this bad until..." She stopped.

"Until what?"

"Caracas." She took a deep breath. "A couple of months ago I was on an assignment there. Things went wrong. I was taken captive and held hostage by a group of would-be revolutionaries." The words came quickly now, tumbling over one another in her need to get them out. "They took me by boat to an island off Caracas. I was bound and gagged, my eyes were covered. I remember the chop of the sea and the wind, the night wind on my face. I remember..."

She gulped for air. He wanted to take her hand but didn't think she would want him to.

"There were three of them. One of them put his hands on me. He tried...all the time I was in the cave he tried to... But the other two men always stopped him."

Thornton moved closer so that his shoulder brushed hers. He wanted to give her his warmth, wanted her to know she wasn't alone.

"When they got me out of the boat that first night, they took the blindfold off and I could see the lights of Caracas in the distance. They took me down the beach away from the landing. It was cold and I was wet from the sea spray. I couldn't see where I was going. I asked them where they were taking me and one of them hit me." She clasped her arms around her legs as though to warm herself, as though she were still cold. "They took me to a sea cave," she said in a shaking voice. "Like this one. They kept me there. They..." She shook her head, unable to go on.

"How long were you there, Rebecca?"

"For two weeks. Over two weeks."

Thornton swore. He reached for her hand and clasped it in his. She didn't pull away.

"The water...the tide...it came in sometimes when I was alone at night. I was bound. I...I never knew how high the tide would come. Once it came to my waist. I thought...I thought I was going to die. I was never dry. I had ulcers on my ankles and on my feet."

"How did you get away?"

"Ed Blakley, he's next in command after Alex, he found me. The people who had kidnapped me were getting ready to move me to another location. Ed and his men had followed them. They rushed into the cave and suddenly it was over."

"What happened then?"

"They took me to a hospital in Caracas, and when I was a little better they flew me to a hospital in the States. I was on recuperative leave when they called me back."

"Because of me?"

Rebecca nodded. "It's my job. It's what I do."

"Why?"

"Why?" She withdrew her hand, and some of the strength came back into her voice. "I'm very good at what I do."

"I'm sure you are."

"I don't usually panic the way I did a few minutes ago."

"I didn't think you did. It took a lot of courage to get me out of that cell in the Presidencia, Rebecca. I'm very grateful."

"We're not home free yet."

"I know that." He shifted so that his back was against the wall of the cave. "But we're going to make it out of here, out of San Sebastian, I mean. Melinda has a birthday next month. I promised myself I'd be there for it."

"Melinda?"

"My daughter. She's going to be eleven."

"Tell me about her," Rebecca said, because the sound of his voice helped to hold back her fear.

Thornton smiled into the darkness. "She's tall for her age and thin, probably because she's on the go all the time."

He chuckled, and it was a nice sound. "She's a ten-year-old whirling dervish, a freckled-faced wood sprite, mischievous, angelic, spicy and sweet. She has long blond hair, and her eyes are as blue as morning glories..." He gave an embarrassed laugh. "Sorry, I'm afraid when it comes to my daughter I tend to get carried away."

"No, don't stop. I want to hear." Anything... anything to keep the fear away.

"Mrs. Plum, that's our housekeeper, is teaching Melinda to cook, and Melinda's quite serious about it. The night before I left she fixed meat loaf and baked potatoes."

"That's more than I can do."

"Really? You can't cook?"

"Nope."

"But you fixed breakfast this morning."

"And that's about the extent of my culinary art." She smiled, relaxing a little. "Tell me more about Melinda, Professor."

"Would you mind calling me Tom? Or Thomas?"

"All right. Tom, then. It's a good name. Strong."

He shifted again, trying to get comfortable, and put an arm around her shoulders. She stiffened and he said, "I think we ought to turn the flashlight off, Rebecca. We'll need it later. I just thought we both might feel better if we were closer."

She knew he was right. If the flashlight failed... She braced herself. "Turn it off, Thomas, uh, Tom." Darkness enveloped them. "Tell me..." She swallowed hard. "Tell me about where you live."

"Brookfield Falls." He tightened his arm around her shoulder. "Population fifty-six hundred. I was born and brought up there. Married my high school sweetheart."

"What was her name?"

"Beth, Beth McGovern. She died when Melinda was five."

"And you've never remarried?"

"No, I haven't. Melinda and I live in what used to be my grandparents' home. It's an old white house, more than a hundred years old, with gray shingles and a blue door. It's probably too big for just the two of us, but I wouldn't give it up for anything in the world.

"It's on a tree-lined street not far from the river and only a fifteen-minute walk to the college. I like it best in the fall when all the big maples along the street start to change and you can feel the crunch of dry leaves under your feet. It..." He laughed and shook his head. "I'm talking too much. Tell me about yourself. Where did you grow up?"

"In a high-rise apartment in New York City. Mostly my view of trees was from the forty-second floor overlooking Central Park." She tried to see his face through the terrible darkness but couldn't. "Different backgrounds."

"Yes, different."

She could hear the sound of the waves. What if they came higher? she thought. What if they rush in and the tide rises so high we can't get out? She took a steadying breath. "Tell me more about your home," she murmured.

He felt the rigid stiffness of her body and knew how frightened she still was. "There are lilacs in the summer in almost all of the backyards. We have big bushes of them in our yard. Violets and lily of the valley grow all along the side of the house, and last summer Melinda planted daisies and marigolds. She planted radishes, too, but they never came up."

He drew her closer. "All the trees along the river begin to grow green and heavy with buds in the spring, the willows and the box elder, the red ash tress. And the dogwood blooms. You should see it then, after the winter when everything is fresh and new. It's like the world stirs and wakens. It's like..."

And little by little as he talked about the place he so obviously loved, her fear, like the slowly ebbing tide, receded. Her eyes drifted closed and she slept.

He held her as he would hold Melinda when she was afraid. A smile played across his lips, because from what little he had seen of Rebecca Bliss, he knew she thought of herself as a tough, competent professional. And she was. But now he knew that beneath that tough exterior there was a vulnerable woman, a woman he could relate to, not in a chauvinist way, but as a man. That pleased him.

He thought about her being held in a cave like this one, bound and helpless, and tightened his arms around her. She murmured in her sleep and he said, "It's all right, Rebecca. Sleep now. Everything's all right."

She burrowed closer against his shoulder, not wanting to awaken from the dream. She was in a field of lavender lilacs and she was running, not away from something, but toward something, joyfully eager because something . . . somebody waited for her there beneath the maple trees. He—

"Rebecca?" Thornton shook her. "Wake up, Rebecca. It's daylight. We have to leave."

Her eyelids fluttered. "Dreaming," she murmured.

"I hope it was a nice dream."

She opened her eyes and looked up at him. "It was nice. Where . . . ?" Her eyebrows came together in consternation. "We're in the cave. We—"

"It's getting light outside. We should leave."

She moved away from him, conscious now that her head had rested on his shoulder, that his arms had been around her. "Did you . . . ?" She was embarrassed. "Were you able to sleep?"

"Yes, I slept." He stood and stretched, easing his muscles, and pointed toward the light at the opening of the cave. "We'd better get moving."

They picked up the backpacks and went toward the entrance. "Wait here." He put a cautioning hand on her arm. "Let me make sure it's okay."

"That's my job." She brushed his hand away and stepped outside. It was barely light. Mist rose from the sea, waves rippled in toward shore. The beach was deserted. "All right. You can come out."

He came, but he was angry, and damned if she was going to tell him what to do every step of the way.

"We'll check the Jeep," she said.

"They'd have cleaned it out by now."

"Maybe." She started toward the rocks; Tom had no choice but to follow her.

He was right—the Jeep had been stripped. Rebecca muttered under her breath and began looking beneath the seats. She found two apples. "Breakfast," she said, and tossed one of them to him.

They crossed the beach and headed for the trees. When they were well back from the road, she stopped and took a map out of her backpack. "The Plantation was about ten miles back," she said, studying it. "Villa Nova is here." She pointed. "Between fifteen and twenty miles inland. We should be able to make it before dark if we..." She stopped. Then, frowning at Thornton, asked, "What are you doing?"

He took a can of tuna and a package of crackers out of his backpack and settled down on his haunches under a tree. "I'm going to have breakfast. I've been on a prison diet for a long time. I can walk the twenty miles, but not on an empty stomach."

Rebecca bit into her apple and glared at him.

"Want some tuna?"

"No."

"Suit yourself." He took a plastic fork out of the small package of utensils and began to eat. When he was finished, he wiped the fork off and put it back in the package, then raked the leaves and a portion of earth aside and buried the empty can.

Mouth tight with impatience, she looked at the compass she'd dug out of her pack. "This way," she snapped, and started off through the trees.

She had no idea why he was angry. He'd been different last night. She'd liked listening to him talk about his daughter and his home. She'd been comforted by his voice, and she'd liked having his arms around her. But this morning he was behaving like a bear with a burr in his paw, and she didn't know why.

She'd be glad when this was over, when they found the missile site and got the pictures. This was day six. They had four more days before the rendezvous with the pickup boat.

Four days. She worried about their supplies. When they found the Jeep stripped, she had checked both backpacks. His held only a few cans of tuna, some crackers, a bag of fruit, and the two bottles of water. She had a couple of T-shirts, the camera, a tape recorder, the compass and her gun. Her money, ID and credit cards were in a separate compartment, wrapped in cellophane.

The day grew hotter. The thickness of trees and heavy underbrush made the going difficult. She wished she'd worn jeans last night instead of shorts, because the bushes were scratching her bare legs.

Thornton had good legs—long, straight, muscular. Good buns, too—tight and firm. She averted her eyes. Great legs and buns aside, she had to concentrate on getting them out of here and back to Washington. It was obvious that his ordeal had taken a great deal out of him. She hoped he was up to what lay ahead.

They went on without speaking, deeper into the trees. Her legs ached and her back was tired, but she made herself go on for another mile before she said, "Let's take a break."

He took one of the bottles of water out and handed it to her. "A canteen would have been easier."

"They were in the Jeep." She took a swig of the water and handed it back to him.

"You'd better eat something," he said.

"I'm all right. We don't have too much. I'll wait until later."

"Maybe I can find some fruit. Stay put." He turned and disappeared into the trees before Rebecca had time to object.

She sat down, leaning against a tree and closed her eyes. They'd made maybe five miles; they still had a long way to go. She could do it; she'd done it before. But could he?

He came back in a few minutes, his shirt off, using it as a sack to carry the mangoes he'd found. "Lunch," he said, and sat on the ground across from her.

Rebecca ate one without speaking. When she was finished, she asked, "Why are you angry? You weren't last night. Last night you were . . . nice."

Thornton wiped his mouth with the back of his hand. "You were nice, too. Last night."

"Meaning that I wasn't this morning?"

"That's right." He reached for another mango. "I know you're doing your job, Rebecca, and I'm more grateful than I can ever tell you for getting me out of that hellhole of a prison. But I don't like being ordered about. I don't like being told what to do."

"I'm trained to do what I do. I'm a professional. I—"

"I know that and I respect what you do, but I don't want you treating me like a damn idiot."

She stiffened and her mouth thinned. "That wasn't my intention."

"Maybe it wasn't, but that's what it seemed like." He took a bite of the fruit. When he swallowed it, he said, "Look, we have to work together if we want to get out of here in one piece. I don't think you like me very much, and I'm not sure I like you. But for as long as we're on the island we've got to try to get along. Agreed?''

"Agreed." She met his gaze, her eyes serious. "Whatever you think about me, Thornton, I *am* a professional and I know what I'm doing. If I tell you to do something, I want you to do it because how you act and react just might save our lives." She hesitated, then held out her hand and said, "I'm sorry if I've been abrupt. I'm afraid it's a habit of mine. I'll try to do better. All right?"

"Fair enough." He took her hand. And knew that though not much had been settled, they had reached a truce of sorts. He stood and hefted the backpack. "We'd better get going."

They stopped again three hours later. They ate some of the crackers, shared one of the larger mangoes and drank a little of the water. It was so hot that their sweat-stained shirts clung to their backs. Thornton was tired, but not as tired as he'd thought he would be. He'd slept okay last night and he'd had a couple of good meals since they'd left San Sebastian. He could feel his strength returning and knew he'd be able to keep up.

When they pushed on, the brush and the trees became thicker, the terrain more difficult. They began to climb, and when they came to a patch of ground where the trees were thinner, they could see the volcano.

"Montaña de Fuego," Rebecca said. "The Mountain of Fire."

"Then we're not too far from Villa Nova. It's only a village, but we might be able to pick up some supplies there."

"How big a place is it? Would they have telephones or telegraph?"

"I doubt it."

"Then we can take a chance that they don't know about us. How far is it to the missile site from there?"

"Another five or six miles."

Rebecca looked at her watch. "It's almost four. Maybe we can still make it before dark."

It took them twenty minutes to reach the village. It was little more than one long dirt street with a few shacks, a *farmacia,* and a hole-in-the-wall grocery store.

They went into the store. The man behind the cluttered counter looked at them curiously. "You folks lost?" he asked.

Rebecca shook her head. "My husband is a biologist," she said as Thornton began looking around. "He's doing research on plant and animal life here in San Sebastian."

"Plants be plants," the man said. "And we don't have too much animal life. Only rabbits, squirrels, coons and some cougars. No snakes. Mongoose came in a long time ago and wiped 'em out." He scratched his whiskered face. "How far you be going?"

"To St. Catherine's," Rebecca said, remembering the name on the map. "Then back to Illinois. That's where we're from."

Thornton raised an eyebrow. She'd probably never set foot in the state and very likely never would. He picked out two cans of beans, some potted meat and a box of crackers. There wasn't any bottled water. "Do you have beer?" he asked.

"Yes, sir." The man reached behind him, put two beers on the counter and opened them.

They were warm, but they were wet. That was all that mattered.

The storekeeper figured up the total, and Thornton, because he had no money, said, "Pay the man, dear."

She shot him a look and answered in a honeyed tone, "Of course, darling." And had the satisfaction of catching his sudden look of surprise.

When they left the village, they began to climb higher into the mountains. Though the going was rough, the air was cooler and they made good time.

As they drew closer, Thornton said, "We veer to the right. I don't think it's too far now." He stopped, scanning the region, wishing he had his binoculars. "I remember I passed an overhang of rocks—"

"There?" Rebecca pointed upward.

"Yes." He breathed a sigh of relief. "Yes, that's the place. We have to climb now."

They went almost straight up, clambering over rocks, pulling each other up, trying to find footholds, panting with effort until finally they reached the summit.

"This way," Thornton said in a low voice. He dropped to his hands and knees and began crawling through the tall grass.

Rebecca followed. He stopped. "There it is," he whispered.

She edged closer to the precipice. And saw, far below, the crumbled ruins of what had once been a city. And green-uniformed guards. "Where...?" Then she saw the missile site almost hidden in the midst of jungle growth.

She looked at Thornton, her eyes shining in triumph. "We've found it!"

Chapter 6

Thornton spoke into the tape recorder, noting the terrain, landmarks, number of guards posted, accessibility and the visible number of launchers. Rebecca took the photographs. They worked quickly, quietly, a team now, each with their own thoughts about the potential for death if the missiles were ever put into operation. Aware too of the danger to their own lives if they were discovered.

But even though she was aware of the danger, and horrified that there actually were missiles here on this Caribbean island, Rebecca felt a zing of triumphant excitement. They'd found the base, and what was more, they had proof it was here in San Sebastian. The information was vital; they had to get it off the island.

She darted a look at the setting sun. "It'll be dark in another thirty minutes," she whispered. "Are you finished?"

Tom nodded. Remembering the last time he'd been in this same spot, he said, "The sooner we're out of here the better I'll like it."

They scuttled backward on their hands and knees, then rose. Bending low, they ran toward the rocks and began the precarious climb down to tree level. They climbed without speaking except when he said, "Here, give me your hand. Careful now."

When they were once again in the shelter of the trees, she grinned and said, "We did it! Mission accomplished."

Her face was dirty. She'd skinned one knee and torn her shorts. Wisps of red hair that she'd pulled back into a ponytail this morning clung to her sweaty face. He thought of the beautifully dressed, coiffed and sweet-smelling woman who had laughed at him when she passed his cell. He hadn't liked her, but he did like this sweaty, rumpled woman in her torn shorts, her face dirty.

"You look like a ragamuffin," he said.

"Yuck! I bet I even smell." She wrinkled her nose. "I'd give half my kingdom for a bath."

"The first time I came here I passed a small pond. Maybe we can find it."

"Let's try. And we've got to find a place to spend the night . . . Tom."

There was a certain awkwardness in the way she said his name, as though she wasn't sure she should. And she wasn't. Professor Thornton was her assignment; her job was to get him and the film and the taped information safely out of San Sebastian. She didn't want to think of him as Tom, but rather as Professor Thornton, because it was always best in her kind of work not to form any kind of personal attachment to the person she worked with or, in this case, rescued. Any personal feeling could complicate the performance of her duty.

She did, of course, feel an overwhelming relief that they'd found the missile site. That part of her mission had been accomplished, but they weren't out of the woods yet. They still had a long way to go before they were safe. With Feliciano and his men looking for them, they were in danger every step of the way.

"Over here," Thornton said, interrupting her thoughts. He headed into the bush, and minutes later they found the pond, half hidden by leafy-green bamboo and fan palms.

"Wonderful!" It was all Rebecca could do not to rip her clothes off right on the spot. But she made herself ask, hoping Thornton wouldn't say yes, "Would you like to go first?"

"No thanks. You go ahead. I'll look around for a camping spot."

"I won't be long."

"Take your time. We've got all night."

"Okay," she said, and took a bar of soap and a clean T-shirt out of the backpack. The shirt was one she'd bought for him, and it looked as though it were three sizes too large for her. But size didn't matter. All she wanted to be was clean.

"See you in a couple of hours," she joked.

"It had better not be that long, or I'll come in after you." He grinned and turned away. "Enjoy yourself," he said over his shoulder. "I won't be long."

She found herself smiling as she undressed because, after all, the professor wasn't such a bad guy. Certainly he wasn't the wimp she had pictured him to be. He was a strong man, sensitive, a bit irascible, stubborn. That showed in the thrust of his rather handsome chin . . . in his rather handsome face. Yes, she admitted to herself, he *was* a good-looking man. His features told of a Scandinavian background, as did his height and the breadth of his shoulders.

She wondered as she started into the pond why he hadn't married again, and bet that every single woman between nineteen and ninety in that podunk Illinois town where he lived had tried to snare him. So, probably, had most of his female students.

Still thinking about him, Rebecca waded into the water that was refreshingly cool after the heat of the day, and deep enough to swim. She swam for a little while, then came into more shallow water, shampooed her hair and bathed. When that was done, she scrubbed her shorts and shirt, panties and bra. After she left the pond, she hung them on a nearby bush to dry. By the time she'd done that she was almost dry.

She had just pulled the too-big T-shirt over her head when she heard Tom call out, "Hey, there, are you decent?"

"About as decent as I can get," she called back.

He pushed through the trees. "I found a place . . ." He stopped, staring. Her red hair hung in tangles down her back. The T-shirt clung to her body, and he could see the outline of her nipples peaked from the cool dampness of her shirt. He swallowed hard and tried to avert his gaze. "A place not far from here. We could . . ." He couldn't take his eyes off her. The T-shirt came to midthigh. She had sensational legs. She had everything! Fiery red hair, green eyes, a sensational body and a face, now that he'd really looked at her, so beautiful that it took away his breath.

"Show me," she said.

He looked at her, dazed. "What?"

"The place you've found. Where we're going to camp for the night."

"Oh." Tom rubbed a hand across his face and tried to get his mind off her and onto something else. "Through the trees. There's an outcrop of rocks."

"Okay." Rebecca tossed him the soap and turned away.

He watched her go. One end of her shirt snagged on a low branch. He caught a quick glimpse of bare bottom before she unsnagged it and disappeared into the trees.

He stood motionless, breathing like a man who'd run a twenty-six-mile marathon. Without taking his clothes off he plunged into the pond and ducked his head underwater to try to cool his thoughts. He'd never before felt this kind of raw desire for a woman. It burned through him, hot, demanding. His heart was pounding, his body was taut, as hard as a rock. He tried to think of other things—the university, his students, home, fall when the leaves turned burnished red . . . as red as Rebecca's hair.

He groaned aloud.

Twenty minutes later and somewhat calmer Tom came out of the water. He hung the clothes he'd washed on the bushes next to Rebecca's and tried not to look at the small pink briefs or the lacy bra. He put on his wet briefs and a clean shirt. Then, taking a deep breath, he went through the trees toward the overhang of rocks.

She was sitting cross-legged, head bowed, brushing her hair. When she straightened and tossed her hair back from her face, she saw him. "Hi," she said. "Enjoy the bath?"

"Yes, it was…" His voice cracked. He cleared his throat. "Yeah," he said, starting again. "It was great."

She fastened her hair into a ponytail and rose gracefully. "Dinner's ready," she said, and led the way to the overhang of rocks where earlier he had placed palm leaves and grass for them to sleep on.

The thought of their sleeping there, too close for comfort, unsettled him.

They sat down, a package of crackers and an open can of beans between them. "Wonderful," Rebecca said between bites. "I was starved."

To get his mind off the way she looked and the way he felt, Thornton asked, "What's the plan? I mean about tomorrow. Do you think we should stay here where it's safe for another day or head down the beach toward Grenville?"

"I think we'd better head for the beach. We can stick to the cover of the jungle and still keep the beach in sight. It's at least a two-day walk to Grenville. The meeting place is five miles beyond. We've got to be there on time. The ship won't wait."

"Why not? You risked your neck getting me out of that cell and getting the photographs of the missile site." He was getting mad. "I don't think I like these people you work for. They expect you to do all the dangerous work and they can't wait an extra day or two to pick you up?"

"If we're not at the rendezvous point on the agreed-upon date, they'll wait for three hours," she said patiently. "If we don't show, they'll leave and try again in two days. They'll follow that pattern until we show up or…"

He looked at her. "Or what?"

"Or they know we're not going to."

His face tight, he asked, "Why do you do it?"

"Because it's my job."

"There are other jobs."

"Not like this one." She shook her head. "I don't think I could manage a safe nine-to-five job, Tom. I need to feel like I'm doing something that's important."

"And dangerous?"

She nodded. "I like the challenge."

"But you didn't like what happened to you in Caracas."

She lowered her gaze. He saw her hand tighten around the plastic fork. "No, I didn't like that."

"It could happen again."

"It won't. I was careless in Caracas. Besides, after this job I'm going to take a couple of months off. Hayden promised me I could."

"What about your folks? What do they think about the kind of work you do?"

"My dad doesn't really know what I do. My mother's dead." She put the empty can aside and reached for a mango. "She was an actress, Lydia Farrow. She—"

"Lydia Farrow!" Thornton's eyes widened. "I remember her. She was one of the most beautiful women I've ever seen. I still see her once in a while in an old movie on television. She won an Academy Award for..." He shook his head. "I can't remember."

"*Winter White,* with Vincent Sortelli."

"Were you and your mother close?"

"No. I really only saw her once. When I was six. She was in New York doing a play. Before she went back to Hollywood she said she'd send for me at Christmas time. But she didn't."

A moment ago she'd sounded tough and competent. Just now she'd looked like a little girl lost, someone he wanted to put his arms around and comfort. In his mind's eye he saw the child who had waited in vain for a Christmas visit with her mother.

She bit into a mango. "Sweet," she said, and swiped at the juice that ran down her chin.

Now, along with wanting to hold her, came the sudden urge to lick the juice off her chin, to kiss her full lips, to... He bit into the mango. Get hold of yourself, Thornton, he told himself. This isn't a woman you could possibly be interested in.

But, Lord, how fine it would be to make love to her.

She finished the mango and wiped her hands on the grass. "That should hold us till morning," she said cheerfully, and started to her feet. But when she did she murmured, "Ouch."

"What is it?"

"Nothing. Just my knee."

"Better let me have a look at it."

"It's all right, really."

He reached into the bag and took out the first-aid kit. "Sit down," he ordered.

She did, obediently stretching her leg out. Her long, beautifully shaped, tanned leg.

Thornton reached for the antiseptic cream. "I'll try not to hurt you."

"It's a scraped knee."

But when he touched her skin with the cream, she flinched.

"Easy," he said, gentling her with his other hand around the calf of her leg. "I'm just going to clean it."

She gripped the material of the T-shirt between her legs, suddenly conscious she had nothing on beneath the shirt. And aware, so very aware of his touch against her skin. A warning bell went off in her brain and she tightened her grip on the material.

"There," he said. "I'll take care of the clean up. You'd better rest that knee."

"Okay." Rebecca cleared her throat. "Thanks."

"Don't mention it." He smiled. "Be back in a couple of minutes."

She was alone in the growing darkness. Night birds sang in the trees above them, and palm fronds moved in a rustling breeze. She lay back. Between the branches of the trees she could see the stars. It was so quiet here, so utterly peaceful. The tensions and the dangers of the day had eased. They were safe, at least for now. And in a strange way that was all that mattered. She was clean, and safe, and with Tom Thornton.

He was different from other men she had known, men like her father who were in the entertainment business. Even than men like Alex Hayden and Ed Blakley. Certainly different from the type of man she usually dated. There was something about Tom Thornton that exuded a quiet dignity and strength. She couldn't imagine him ever doing anything dishonest or dishonorable. He wasn't at all the kind of man she had thought he would be.

He came through the trees, a silhouetted shadow in the darkness, and Rebecca smiled because she was glad she was here with him and not with someone else.

He settled onto the ground beside her. "Sorry we don't have a blanket."

"We don't need it. It's a nice night."

"Tired?"

"Yes. You?"

"Yeah, but a good tired." He lay back, conscious of her beside him. All he had to do was reach out his hand and—

"I guess we'd better get some sleep," she said.

"I guess so."

"Good night, Professor."

"Good night, Rebecca."

He lay with his eyes open, looking up at the stars, his body rigid with desire, more aware of her than he'd ever been of any other woman. And painfully aware of the fact that she had nothing on under the shirt. All he'd have to do...

He looked over at her. She lay with her arms behind her head, unaware how the shirt stretched across her chest or that in the dim light he could see the rise and fall of her breasts, the enticing nubs of her nipples.

Smothering a groan, Tom rolled onto his back away from her. He didn't relax until he heard her even breathing and knew that she slept.

A bird song, shrill and imperious, woke Tom. He lay for a few moments, orienting himself to his surroundings before he opened his eyes and looked toward Rebecca. She was on her side with her back to him, her head resting on her hands. The shirt was pulled up, revealing one round, firm cheek.

Still half asleep, he rested a hand on her bare bottom and began to gently caress her.

"Umm," she murmured, and wiggled closer.

He had an instant reaction. He knew he should stop, but her skin was satin smooth and cool beneath his hand. He closed his eyes, continuing to caress her, smiling at her barely audible snore, the small sleepy sounds of pleasure as she began to awaken. He told himself he would stop before she fully awakened. In one more moment he would.

He felt her body stiffen beneath his hand, heard her smothered gasp before she turned. "What are you...?" She yanked the shirt down over her hips as she turned. "You...you were touching me," she sputtered.

"Couldn't help it." Tom opened his eyes.

"You most certainly could have."

"Perhaps." His lips twitched in a smile. "You have a lovely derriere, Miss Bliss."

"Really, Professor Thornton!"

"Tom."

She glared at him. "You took advantage of me while I was half asleep."

"I was half asleep, too, if that's any excuse." He leaned on one elbow and looked down at her. "I'm sorry if I offended you. It just seemed..." He tucked a strand of hair behind her ear. "You're a very beautiful woman, Rebecca. Especially now, like this. On a morning like this."

Before she knew that he intended to he leaned forward and kissed her, gently, softly.

Her lips were still under his. She didn't respond, but she didn't move away.

He raised his face from hers and looked down at her, his eyes intent, puzzled. "Sorry," he said. "I'll try not to let that happen again." Then he got up and went through the trees in the direction of the pool.

Rebecca sat up and hugged her knees. She ran her tongue over her lips as though to taste him. Then she shook her head, as angry at herself as she was with him.

Thirty minutes later, after they both bathed and dressed separately, they left the place where they had slept.

It was a little after noon when they heard the patrol. They had stopped in a clearing to eat a meager lunch of crackers and fruit when Rebecca held up a cautioning hand.

"What is it?" he asked. "What—?"

She motioned him to silence and pointed back the way they had come. Backpacks in hand, they crawled toward a cluster of bushes. There, flat against the ground, hidden by the leafy plants, barely daring to breathe, they heard the voices and the sound of branches snapping.

"This way, *Sargento,*" a man said. "Over here."

Another voice cursed and muttered, "This is ridiculous. They wouldn't have come this far into the jungle."

"The *commandante* said we were to search every piece of ground within a five-mile radius of the base," someone else said. "If they've come this way, I mean to find them. Spread out and search every inch of ground."

Rebecca raised her head. She saw boots, the blue of army pants.

"What will we do when we find them?" a man asked.

"Turn them over to General Feliciano, of course."

"He will kill them?"

"Most assuredly he will kill the man."

"And the woman?"

One of them laughed. "He has something else planned for her. It's whispered that she outsmarted him before she released the man from the prison in the Presidencia. The general will kill her for that, but not until she has suffered sufficiently and is of no more use to him."

Tom turned his head so that he could see Rebecca. She looked grim but not frightened. He put his hand over hers and squeezed it.

A swarm of mosquitoes buzzed around their heads. A small rodent moved cautiously closer, but neither Rebecca nor Tom moved.

Time passed. The voices came and went, sometimes closer, sometimes farther away. When at last the voices receded, Rebecca raised her head. "They've gone," she whispered, and slowly, cautiously, they moved from their hiding place.

"We'd better get the hell out of here," he whispered.

"Yes . . ." Her eyebrows came together in a frown. She placed a warning hand on his arm. "Wait," she cautioned. "Something—"

A man with sergeant's stripes on his sleeves, his rifle pointed directly at them, stepped from behind the trees. "I knew it," he said triumphantly. "I had a feeling the two of you were close by. *¡Manos arriba!* Quickly! Hands over your heads."

"Listen," Rebecca said, "we'll pay you. I have money, American money. I—"

"*¡Callete!* Shut up!" With his rifle he motioned them toward the clearing. "I'll get a promotion when I turn you in. That's a hundred times more valuable than money." He reached into his shirt pocket and pulled out a silver whistle.

"A lot of money," Rebecca said.

He put the whistle to his lips, then hesitated.

"Ten thousand dollars."

"Ten—*carumba,* that is..." Mosquitoes circled over his head. He put one hand up to brush them away, and when he did, Tom rushed him. Moving fast, head down, he knocked the sergeant to the ground, grabbed the rifle and, before the man could cry out, hit him with the rifle butt.

"*¡Sargento! ¿Que pasa?* What's happening? Where are you?" a voice cried out from somewhere behind them.

Tom yanked the bandolier from around the soldier's chest. "Come on!" he muttered.

And together they raced for the trees.

Chapter 7

She ran hard, heart drumming a frantic beat in her chest. They were closing in. It was like Caracas. Dear God...pain in her side, hard to breathe... She stumbled, tried to save herself, fell.

Behind her voices called out, "Don't let them get away!"

She struggled up, eyes wide with remembered terror.

Thornton gripped her arm. "Come on," he cried. He grabbed her hand to help her up, and suddenly she knew that this time it was different. This time she wasn't alone.

Together they raced through the tangle of trees and underbrush. Limbs struck their faces, thorns scratched and bloodied them, but they ran on. Ahead of them they saw a clearing, and the mountain, rocky, high, dangerous. If they could reach the mountain, they had a chance to lose themselves among the rocks.

They ran toward it, heard a gunshot, a shouted order.

They reached the edge of the clearing. Rebecca hesitated. They'd be vulnerable there, exposed. She shot a glance at Thornton. "It's the only way," he said, grabbing her hand as he raced with her across the clearing.

Fear spurred her on, gave strength to aching muscles, to the pain in her side. At the base of the mountain they began to climb, keeping low, reaching for handholds, breathing hard.

Rebecca hung on to the ledge of a rock. "Let me catch my breath," she panted.

He pulled her behind the rock and looked down. The soldiers hadn't reached the clearing. But they would soon. He gave her a minute before he said, "We have to go on."

"Okay," she murmured. "Okay."

She climbed, ignoring skinned knuckles and broken fingernails, aware that any minute now the soldiers would find the clearing. The backpack felt as though it weighed fifty pounds. Tom was behind, pushing her up with a hand against her thigh or her bottom. It suddenly occurred to her, in the midst of her physical distress, that she was supposed to be the leader of this expedition. She had come to rescue him, not the other way around. And there was a part of her that resented that, resented him for taking charge.

But what she resented most of all, what disturbed her more than anything else, was that she didn't have the stamina she'd had before Caracas. Her body hadn't recovered from the terrible ordeal she had been through. Alex shouldn't have sent her out so soon again.

She tried harder, pushing herself to the limit of her endurance. Tom Thornton was her responsibility. His life depended on her knowledge and her strength. She couldn't give up. She couldn't let him see her falter.

He pulled her up beside him, then edged around an overhang of rocks and looked down. "Looks like a whole squad of them," he whispered. "We've got to get to the top. We'll be safe there in case they try to come up."

Rebecca looked at the almost sheer face of rock they still had to climb. She wiped a hand across her sweaty face. "Let's go."

Tom took a bottle of water out of one of the packs and handed it to her. She drank and handed it back to him. He took only a sip.

"How're you holding up?" she asked because, after all, he was the one who'd been through hell in that cell they'd locked him up in. "You making it all right?"

"I'm fine. You okay?"

"Sure." She forced a smile. "We'd better get going, partner."

They climbed higher, all the while doing their best to stay in the shadow of the rocks so they wouldn't be seen from below. When they reached the most difficult part, he said, "I've had a little experience with mountain climbing, so let me go first. Try to place your feet and your hands where I do."

Rebecca nodded. He began to inch himself upward, searching with his feet for a niche, an overhang of rock. She knew that her strength was going, but pressed on because she had to. She followed, using the same overhangs, the same niches he had used.

When he reached the top and heaved himself over, she waited, trying to get her breath before that last few difficult feet.

"It's going to be okay," Tom whispered down to her.

She took a deep breath, then found a foothold, reached above to a piece of jutting rock and grasped it. It began to crumble under her fingers. She tried to hold on, to find another niche, something . . .

Thornton lay on his stomach to try to reach her. She looked up and saw the fear in his eyes, saw the sweat running off his face. He grunted with effort and reached for her hand.

The rock crumbled; below lay death.

He grasped her hand. "Easy," he said. "I've got you." And he began to pull her upward, his hand clasping hers, a lifeline, holding her, bringing her ever closer to safety.

She came up, arms and knees scraping the hard surface, up and over. He stood and pulled her into his arms, and she clung to him, sobbing in relief, holding on to his solidness, his strength.

He cupped her face between his hands. "I've got you. You're safe now, Rebecca. Are you okay? Is anything broken?"

She shook her head. "I'm bruised, battered, but unbowed," she said in a shaky voice. Then, ashamed of her fear, she made herself smile and say, "You're stronger than you look, Professor. Thanks."

A muscle jumped in his cheek. "My pleasure, ma'am." He looked her up and down. "You really are bruised and battered."

"Nothing that a soak in a hot tub and three weeks in Bermuda won't cure."

She moved out of his embrace, and he found himself wishing she hadn't because he liked the feel of her in his arms. He'd been more afraid than he'd ever been in his life when the rock crumbled beneath her fingers. He'd pulled her up, muscles straining, praying for strength, and when he had her in his arms, he hadn't wanted to let her go.

She stood away from him, back from the edge so that the soldiers below wouldn't be able to see them. "I wish I knew where we were. But wherever we are, I'm glad it's up here and not down there." She looked at him. "You handled yourself pretty well back there, Professor. You surprised me."

It was the second time in the past couple of minutes that she'd called him "Professor." He didn't like it. There was something in the way she said it, a put-down in her voice that made him mad.

He took a step forward and gripped her shoulders. "My name is Tom, Rebecca, and if you call me 'Professor' one more time, I'm going to throw you off this mountain."

He glared at her, and before she could step away he kissed her the way he'd wanted to ever since yesterday when he saw her come out of the pool wearing only a too-big T-shirt.

She tried to struggle out of his grasp, but he held her, one arm around her waist, the other against the back of her head. He kissed her with all of the pent-up emotion he was feeling—fear and anger and desire. Oh, yes, desire. Because he wanted her. Wanted to take her down on the ground and make wild and urgent love to her.

He kissed her hard, not the way he'd ever kissed a woman before. She protested and cried, "Let me go!

Let me—'' And he took her bottom lip between his teeth. She gasped, and when her lips parted his tongue sought hers, insistent, demanding.

She tried to wriggle out of his grasp, and he pressed one hand against the small of her back to bring her closer. He kissed her, savagely, hungrily. She moaned low in her throat, and suddenly she was answering his kiss, her tongue touching his, and she was holding him as he was holding her, her body close, moving against his in an urgency that matched his own.

"Rebecca," he whispered against her lips. "Rebecca."

She dropped her head against his shoulder, quivering, gasping for breath. "We . . . we can't do this. You shouldn't have. We—"

"I've wanted to kiss you since yesterday. Since last night." He shook his head. "I could barely keep my hands off you last night."

The slightest suggestion of a smile curved her mouth. "You didn't quite."

"No, I didn't, did I?" He brushed his lips against hers and tightened his arms around her. He kissed her again, more gently this time, and let her go because he knew that if he didn't stop now he wouldn't stop at all. This wasn't the time or the place; they had to get out of here.

She smoothed her hands down over her wrinkled shorts. Her lips looked swollen, her eyes heavy, slumberous.

"Don't look at me like that," he said in a low voice.

A hand fluttered against her throat. She wet her lips, and with that one gesture, the sight of that moist pink tongue darting out to touch her full lower lip, his control almost slipped. He said her name, "Rebecca," and took a step toward her.

She shook her head, picked up her backpack, turned and started away from the rocky plateau.

He waited for a moment, watching her, his shoulders bunched with the effort of holding himself back. He wanted to make love to her, with her. Wanted to feel her body under his, yielding to him, whispering his name in passion and desire. He wanted...

He took long, shaky breaths to try to get his emotions under control, and as he turned to follow her, he remembered the way he'd felt about her during those first few days after she had freed him. As grateful as he'd been to her for rescuing him, he'd thought of her as a hard-as-nails, domineering female, certainly the last woman on earth he'd ever want to know more intimately. Cynically he had imagined how it must be for the poor male who would be fool enough to want to make love to her, imagined the way she would have taken charge and given orders. "Do this!" he'd imagined her saying. "No, no! Not *that* way!"

But now he knew it wouldn't be like that. He'd known how it would be since her lips had parted under his and he had felt the warmth of her body pressing so sweetly to his. His body ached with need as he watched her tall, slim figure move toward the trees.

Tonight, he promised himself. We'll be together tonight.

With the aid of the compass they headed due north toward the sea. When they stopped to study one of the maps, she said, "We'll follow the coastline until we get to Grenville."

She had no idea how far away they were or how long it would take them to get to Grenville. They'd lost precious time, and she didn't think they would be able to make the rendezvous. She had told Tom that if they didn't make the first rendezvous, the ship would return in two days, but she knew that the longer they stayed on the island the greater the chance of their being caught.

"The men we got away from today will send word back that they've seen us," she said. "They have a better idea of where we are now. We'll have to be careful. We won't be able to go near a village because by now word will have spread and there'll be search parties out all over the island. We have enough food to last us for a couple of days, but we're going to need water. That's my fault. I shouldn't have left the canteen behind in the Jeep."

"You did your best, Rebecca. You did more than anyone else could have done when you broke me out of the Presidencia." He gave her a warm smile. "I can see now why they sent you. Nobody else could have gotten close to General Feliciano the way you did."

He remembered then that the soldiers had said they would kill him, but they would save Rebecca for Feliciano. And he knew he would do whatever he had to to keep that from happening, to keep the general from ever laying a hand on Rebecca again.

Had he laid a hand on her? Tom wondered. What lengths had she gone to to get what she wanted? She'd gone up to his quarters. What had happened there before she had given him the knockout drops? Had she let him kiss her? Touch her. Had she . . . ?

He thought then about all of the times the guards had taken him to Feliciano's office and held him there, his arms tied behind his back. He remembered Feliciano's smile. "Ah, you have brought the American for another little chat," he would say. "I hope for his sake that today he's more communicative."

He would get up from behind his desk. "Why don't you tell us the truth, Professor Thornton? Confess that you're SIS. Tell us why you came to San Sebastian."

"I'm not SIS," he'd say for the hundredth time. "I've told you. I'm a history professor. I came to San Sebastian to find the remnants of the aboriginal..."

The signal would be given by the lift of an eyebrow, the slight motion of the hand that held the black cigar, and they would start in on him, battering, beating, bending him double with pain. When they stopped, Feliciano would say, "Once again, Professor. Tell me the truth."

He would flick the ash off the cigar, then inhale till the end was burning red. "Tell me your real reason for coming to San Sebastian," he'd say. And he'd press the burning end of the cigar to Thornton's chest.

Tom had never hated anyone the way he hated Maximo Feliciano. And the thought of that man, that bastard, ever laying a hand on Rebecca made him almost physically ill. If he ever saw the general again, if he ever had the chance, he would kill him with his bare hands. That wasn't a threat; it was a promise.

It was almost dark when they found the mountain stream. The water was icy cool and clean as it filtered down the mountain slope. They drank their fill, then filled the water bottles.

"We can camp here tonight." Rebecca smiled. "I don't know why I say 'camp.' We don't have a tent or even a bedroll."

"We'll manage. We did last night." Tom pointed to a place under the trees. "How about there? Does that suit you?"

It was a pretty spot, an oasis of quiet in a jungle setting, where scarlet hibiscus grew wild and purple bougainvillea climbed high into the tamarind trees. Spanish moss hung from banyan trees, silver and ghostly in the faint light of the rising moon.

"It'll do." And because she was suddenly uncomfortable, Rebecca said, "I'd like to wash up. Would you mind?"

"No, go ahead. I'll see what I can forage in the way of fruit." He smiled at her discomfiture, and knew that in spite of his promise to himself that tonight he would make love to her, he wouldn't unless it was something she wanted, too.

But as Tom searched for and found a mango tree, loquats and guava, his thoughts turned again and again to Rebecca, and how it would be if . . . no, not if but when they made love.

The night was soft and full of promise. The scent of wild jasmine perfumed the air. The moon was yellow-bright.

Rebecca had bathed and changed into the shirt she had washed yesterday and a clean pair of shorts.

She had been more disturbed than she wanted to admit by the way Tom had kissed her earlier today and by her response. She had tried to tell herself that the kiss they had shared had been nothing more than a reaction to their having come safely through a frightening situation. True, he had been angry because she had called him "Professor," but that alone hadn't accounted for his pulling her into his arms. No, she told herself, the kiss and her reaction to it had been nothing more than relief after a terrifying ordeal.

It most certainly mustn't happen again. It was her responsibility to get Thornton—that was the way she would think of him now—safely out of the country. He was an assignment. A personal involvement would endanger both of them. She couldn't let that happen.

And yet when they sat cross-legged under the tamarind tree, eating the fruit he had found, a feeling of pleasant lethargy crept over Rebecca. A breeze, soft as a lover's kiss, gentled through the leaves of the tree. The scent of the jungle, musky humid in the night air, closed in about them, holding them in this small world of their own. It was as though for this short space of time nothing else existed.

She bit into a mango, that most succulent of all fruits, and when she made as though to wipe the juice off her lips, Tom leaned forward. "Let me," he said, and before Rebecca could stop him he began to lick the juice off her mouth.

"Sweet," he murmured. "So sweet."

Her lips tasted of mango, and of her. He delved deeply, tasting the silky warmth of her mouth. When he let her go, he held another piece of fruit to her lips. "Taste it so I can taste you."

As though mesmerized by his voice, she did as he asked, and didn't move away when he began to kiss her again, one hand against the back of her neck to bring her closer while he sampled the mango from her lips.

She had never been kissed like this before, never been warmed by lips as tender as his. She felt as though she were melting into him, her body fluid, her limbs weak. Her lips parted under his, seeking as he sought, tasting as he tasted.

He placed her against the soft jungle moss and raised her shirt. Taking the half-eaten mango, he rubbed it on her breasts. And when she quivered under his touch and asked, "What . . . what are you doing?" he began to lick the mango off her breasts, first one then the other, lapping, circling closer and ever closer to a poised and waiting peak. And when he closed his teeth on one and began to gently suckle, she cried out with a pleasure that left her breathless.

He gentled her with his hands, content for now to kiss her this way, to feel the frantic beat of her heart beneath his hand. "Soon, Rebecca," he said against her flesh.

"No," she whispered. "We shouldn't . . . we can't do this, Tom. We—"

"Yes, we can," he said. He opened the zipper on her shorts. She sucked in her breath, but made no move to stop him. He pushed the shorts down over her thighs and eased his hands under the silky underpants. He touched her, and the breath caught in his throat because she was so warm and moist and ready. He had promised himself that he would wait, but when he touched her this way he knew he couldn't.

He sat up and tugged her shorts and panties off, then her shirt.

And when she lay before him, naked in the moonlight, a moment passed before he could move or speak. She was breathtaking, a woman in every sense of the word, delicate, shapely, beautiful. He rested his hand against her stomach. "You're lovely," he whispered. "You're so unbelievably lovely."

For the first time in her life she was glad she was beautiful. For him.

He kissed her mouth again, then quickly took his clothes off, lay beside her, and pulled her into his arms. It was heaven to hold her like this, to feel the whole silken length of her against his body.

He caressed her breasts, gently drawing the tips out, teasing, lingering while she trembled and opened her body to his. And when she did, he eased his hand down to the apex of her legs and touched her there again. She sighed against his mouth as he began to stroke her, and without his bidding her to she reached to stroke him.

He felt as though his heart would burst. He wanted it to go on forever, but because he knew he couldn't hold himself back any longer, he said, "Now, Rebecca." And rolling her beneath him, he joined his body to hers.

She cried out with the joy of having him inside her, filling her, and she began to move against him, lifting her body to his, matching every movement, every surge, holding him as he held her. He plunged and withdrew, and plunged again, bringing her closer and ever closer to a feeling she had never before experienced. It frightened her, yet she wanted more, oh, yes, please more.

He rained kisses on her face and bent to kiss her breasts. His hands came around her back to draw her closer. His breathing was anguished. She was everything he had ever hoped to find in a woman. She was quicksilver and velvet, fire and lightning.

She couldn't bear this feeling, this wondrous thing that was happening to her. It was too much. She couldn't..."

Suddenly she was out of control, caught up in a frighteningly wonderful vortex of feeling she hadn't thought possible. She heard a cry, a soft, keening moan, and knew it was her own. And his triumphant cry as he took her mouth and his big body thundered over hers, holding her so tightly she could barely breathe.

He said, "Oh, yes. Oh, Becky," and kissed her lips, and held her and soothed her until she was quiet in his arms.

They lay without speaking, their bodies entwined. She looked up at the stars that shone through the trees and felt hot tears of joy sting her eyes because what had happened to her just now had never happened before.

He leaned on one elbow. "What is it? Did I hurt you? What is it, my dear?"

She touched the side of his face. "No, you didn't hurt me. You made me feel..." She shook her head, overcome now by embarrassment.

"What?" he said. "What, Rebecca?"

"I've never...you know." She took a deep breath. "This was the first time I...I ever felt what I felt."

For a moment Tom didn't speak. He looked at her, wonder in his eyes, then he leaned to kiss away the tears that had fallen.

And held her to his beating heart.

Chapter 8

It was still dark when Tom awoke. He lay for a moment, orienting himself to his surroundings before he became aware of Rebecca. She had pressed close to him during the night, one arm around his waist, her face nuzzled against his shoulder. Still half asleep, he put his arms around her and kissed the top of her head.

He had known his average share of women before he'd met and married Beth during his senior year at Michigan. He had loved Beth and he had been faithful to her all through their marriage. There had been a woman or two in his life since her death, but he had steered clear of any emotional involvement.

Now he wondered if that was because he hadn't wanted an involvement or because the relationships had little or no meaning for him. Certainly with none of the women he had known, not even with Beth, had he felt the kind of passionate high he had experienced with Rebecca Bliss.

Bliss. He smiled to himself. That was what he'd experienced all right, pure and simple bliss.

She stretched and moved closer. He felt himself grow hard, and needing to touch her, he began to caress her breasts and to stroke the silky length of her back, the rounded curve of her bottom.

She murmured something unintelligible and pressed her naked body to his. Without opening her eyes she sought his mouth and kissed him as he had kissed her last night.

His hand moved lower, and when he began to stroke her in that most intimate of places, a fire kindled and grew. But still she lay with her eyes closed, loving his touch, the fingers that teased and tortured. Until it became too much, and when it did, she rolled away from him and said, "Come over me, Tom. Come make love with me. Do all the things you did before."

He took her mouth and felt a wondrous joy in the warmth and aliveness of her body under his, in the knowledge that she wanted him as much as he wanted her. He traced the edges of her lips with his tongue. He caressed her breasts and made her wait while he rested his head against her and suckled one sweet and tender peak.

She murmured her pleasure and held him there, stroking his head and his shoulders as she whispered, "So nice, Tom. So nice."

He came up to kiss her lips, and with his mouth still covering hers he entered her, deep and hard, burying the essence of himself into her, crying out his need when he felt her warmth close about him in total acceptance.

"Oh, yes," she whispered. "Yes, Tom." She lifted her body to his, frantic with a need that matched his own.

Rebecca had told herself as she had drifted to sleep last night, still in the throes of the wonderful thing that had happened to her, that very likely it would never happen again. That never again would she experience the rapture she had known last night. But now as she moved with him and became a part of him, sensation after sensation trembled through her body.

And when he moved against her and asked, in a voice strained with all that he was feeling, "Is it too much? Do I hurt you? Am I—?" she silenced his words with a kiss.

"No, you don't hurt me. I love what you do, what you're doing."

He groaned with pleasure and cupped her bottom to lift her closer.

"Yes," she whispered against his throat. "Like that. Oh, Tom . . . Tom."

The sound of his name on her lips, her acceptance, her response, triggered a new emotion within him. Something wonderful quivered to life, and he wanted to cry her name aloud and tell her all that he was feeling. He wanted this that they shared to go on forever.

He took her mouth, and it was for her as it had been last night. All of her control slipped, and she clung to him, holding him close while her body rose to meet those final thrusts. And when she cried out, he answered her and held her as though he would never let her go.

In a little while, when their breathing grew calmer, he made as though to move away. "No," she said. "Stay here, with me. Cover me with your body."

He raised himself on his elbows and looked down at her. Her face was luminous in the moonlight. He kissed her eyelids, her cheeks, her mouth, and smoothed the tumbled hair back from her face. "I'm too heavy for you."

"No, I like you like this." She tightened her arms around his back and shifted to a more comfortable position. And when she did she felt him grow. "Oh, my. Oh, my."

He chuckled, feeling pleased with himself. "If you want to get any sleep, you'd better lie still."

She stifled a yawn. "All right," she murmured sleepily. "I'll behave." She kissed him. "For now."

In a little while she felt him relax against her. His breathing steadied, deepened, and he slept. And finally so did she, comforted by his weight and by his breath against her throat.

Neither of them knew what would happen today. But for now she was safe in the shelter of his arms.

When Rebecca awoke the next morning, she was alone. She lay for a few minutes, looking up at the trees, listening to a symphony of bird songs. Her body felt light, cleansed, and though she knew she should be up, she didn't move because she wanted to luxuriate in this totally new feeling.

She thought about Tom, and a smile played across her lips. He made her feel . . . it was hard to describe. Fulfilled? Yes, certainly. But it was more than that, so much more. He had made her feel womanly, treasured, one with every woman who had loved.

Her eyes widened. Loved? Surely not. Love didn't have anything to do with what had happened between them last night. The danger they had been in yesterday had sharpened their emotions. That was why they had been drawn together. That was all it was. Great sex. When this was over, she would go back to her life and Tom Thornton would go back to his. The only thing they had in common was the danger they were in.

She got up then, and not bothering with her shorts, she pulled the T-shirt over her head and headed in the direction of the mountain stream to bathe. When she came through the trees, she saw Tom at the edge of the stream, pulling the wet briefs up over his legs. She stopped and watched him sluice water over his face, shoulders and chest. The sun glinted off his body. Water dripped from his hair.

The breath caught in her throat, and the same fire she had known last night kindled and grew. Lust, she told herself. Plain old-fashioned lust.

She stepped out of the trees and went toward him. "Good morning," she called out.

"Morning." He smiled, and something inside her gave way—a funny, fluttery feeling that made the blood rush to her head and her knees go weak.

"Better let me take care of those scratches," he said.

Rebecca shook her head. "They're all right."

He held his hand out to her. "I wish you could see yourself this morning, all sleepy-eyed and rumpled." He took her hand and brought her closer. "You have the most glorious hair," he said, and buried his face in it.

She nuzzled against his shoulder and ran her hands across his bare chest. When she did, he winced and tried to smother a hiss of pain.

"What is it?" she asked, startled.

"Nothing. Sorry."

She stepped away and saw the raw and ugly marks she hadn't seen before. Her stomach knotted as though with pain. "Tom?" she managed to say. "What . . . ? What happened?"

"Feliciano." He took a deep, steadying breath because the memory of it brought a sickness deep in his gut. "He likes cigars. He uses them when he questions people."

Rebecca stared at him, then her gaze lowered to his chest. "Dear God," she whispered. "Dear God."

"It's all right," he said harshly. "It's over now. It doesn't matter."

"It matters." She leaned her face against his chest carefully so that she wouldn't hurt him. And very gently she kissed the places where he had been burned.

"Rebecca . . . ?" He touched her hair. "Don't. They're so ugly. So—"

"Shh," she said against his skin, and she kept kissing him, trying to take away the hurt, filled with a tenderness she hadn't known she possessed.

Tom tightened his hands in her hair. No one had ever touched him as she did. He felt her kisses and her tears, and something so much bigger than passion stirred within him. He wanted her, but there was a difference in the wanting, something deeper, better.

He put his hands on the sides of her head, his fingers tangling in her hair, and lifted her face so that he could kiss her. "Come," he said against her lips, then took her hand and led her toward the trees.

He kissed her again when they reached the cool green jungle. Then, stepping away from her, he hooked his thumbs under the elastic waist of his briefs and eased them down. And watching him, her eyes never leaving his, Rebecca pulled the T-shirt over her head.

He took her back into his arms, and they stood that way, letting passion wait while they held each other. He kissed her again tenderly, deeply, and taking her hand, led her to the place under the trees where they had loved before.

But this time she said, "Let me love you." And when he lay down, she kissed the patches of fatigue under his eyes, his cheeks, the corners of his mouth. His lips twitched, and she kissed his mouth, and as he had done, took his lower lip to tease and to suckle.

Her hands moved down to caress his chest gently, carefully, so that she wouldn't hurt him, down to his flat stomach, over his hips and thighs. She felt his muscles quiver beneath her fingertips as she eased her way through the crisp spring of hair to that hard part of him.

He made himself lie quietly, arms at his sides, while she caressed him. But a shudder ran through his body and he clamped his lower lip between his teeth to keep from crying out. He breathed her name, "Rebecca," and the sound of it on his lips was like a melody. Or a prayer.

He touched her then. He ran his fingers through the softness of her hair. He caressed the curve of her throat, her shoulders and her breasts. She sighed with pleasure, and still caressing him, she rested her head against his stomach.

"Please," he said. "I can't wait. I can't..."

She came up over him and settled herself on him, gasping with pleasure when she began to move against him, slowly at first, then faster, her excitement growing as his grew because she knew she was pleasing him.

That was what she wanted—to please Tom, to give him pleasure. And in the giving she received so much. She leaned forward, her hair splaying across his chest, and took his mouth. He whispered her name against her lips. She whispered his, "Tom, oh, Tom."

Then it became too much, for him and for her, and together they climbed the heights of passion, stayed with it and rode with it until the very end, together, heart beating against heart.

She had little to say as they trudged mile after endless mile down from the mountain toward the beach. This thing between she and Tom Thornton had happened so suddenly. A few days ago he had been only an assignment, a college professor who had stumbled onto information that was vital to the defense of the United States. She hadn't wanted to take this assignment to rescue the man she had referred to as a wimp and an egghead.

She didn't like herself for having said those things. Tom Thornton wasn't a wimp, and if he was an egghead, then more power to him. Yesterday he had proved how strong he was, how brave. His wasn't the chest-thumping, boasting kind of bravery that some men displayed, but rather a quiet strength that proved he could handle himself in any emergency.

She thought of the way he had touched her when they made love, of his infinite gentleness. Earlier today she had tried to tell herself that what passed between them was nothing more than good sex, but she knew now that it was more, that it went so much deeper than that. She had wept this morning when she saw the places where he had been burned, and when she touched him and felt him tremble, it seemed to her that she could feel his pain.

She wanted to kill Feliciano for what he had done to Tom, and she would do anything she had to to keep him safe. Yesterday the soldiers had said that Tom would be killed if he was taken. She had to make sure that didn't happen. She would keep him safe so that he could return to the town that he lived in, to the young daughter that waited for him there.

She thought about the place where he was from and of his life there, and it saddened her because they were so different. She divided her time between an apartment in Arlington and a high-rise New York condo. He lived in Hooterville, Illinois.

But even as she thought the word *Hooterville,* she corrected herself. Tom lived in a place called Brookfield Falls, on a quiet street where the leaves of the trees turned red in the fall. It wasn't her kind of place, but she wouldn't demean it, even in her thoughts, because it was his home.

In the late afternoon they came to a place where they could see the Caribbean stretching for mile after endless mile, turquoise-green and calm in the setting sun. The fishing boats were coming in, and in the distance they could see the gleaming white decks of a luxury liner, a liner that wouldn't call in at San Sebastian.

"We can go down closer to the beach when it gets dark," Rebecca said. "But we'll have to stay within the cover of the trees."

Tom nodded, then followed as she adjusted the backpack on her shoulders and started out again. She had been quiet all day. She'd answered his attempts at conversation with a smile and a brief comment, but it was obvious her thoughts had been elsewhere. He hoped she wasn't sorry about making love, that she wasn't having second thoughts. What had happened between them had been very special. It meant something to him, perhaps more than he wanted to think about at this moment.

When it started to get dark, they found a place near the beach. They made sure there was no one else around, took their clothes off and, hand in hand, waded into the surf. They swam side by side for a long time, then drifted on the crest of the waves, saying little, their bodies touching, hand reaching for hand until darkness came. Only then did they come in toward the shore to stand waist-deep in the moon-silvery water.

He brought her close and kissed her. "You taste of sea. I like that."

She ran a tongue over his lips. "So do I," she murmured.

He ran his hands down her slick, wet body, cupped her breasts and began to kiss them. Her fingers threaded through his sea-wet hair, and she held him there, held him until he picked her up and carried her out of the water to the place where they had left their belongings. There, without a word, they came into each other's arms, lay together and loved together.

Afterward they ate their last can of tuna and almost all of the crackers.

"We still have a can of beans," Rebecca said. "We'll have it for breakfast. We should reach our rendezvous point by tomorrow night." She lay back and looked up at the sky. "Just imagine," she said in a dreamlike voice, "an icy cold martini, a steak that's crisp on the outside and pink in the middle, a baked potato swimming in butter and sour cream.'' She grinned at him. ''How does that sound?''

''A *big* steak,'' he said. ''God knows I need something to keep my strength up.'' He rested a finger against her lips. ''You're going to make an old man out of me, lady.''

''And you're going to have me walking funny, mister.''

He laughed because he liked her bit of bawdiness. He thought about tomorrow when they would meet the rendezvous ship, and there was a part of him that, in spite of the danger they faced here on the island, wanted these days to last. They had known each other for such a short time, and yet Rebecca had become an important part of his life. He couldn't think what it would be like to say goodbye to her.

''You've been quiet today,'' he said. ''Is something wrong?''

''No, of course not. Well...'' She hesitated, and making an excuse for what she was really feeling, said, ''Maybe a case of the jitters, Tom. I think we've outrun Feliciano's boys, but there's still a lot to worry about. We've got to meet the boat and get the film and your notes off the island.'' She looked at him, her eyes serious and loving. ''And most important of all, Professor, we've got to get you to where you're safe.''

She put her arms around him. ''And don't frown at me like you did before when I called you 'Professor,' because I like calling you that.'' She kissed him. ''I wish I'd had a prof like you when I went to college. I'd have stayed after school every day.''

''And I'd have run for the hills if I'd had a student like you in my class. You're dangerous to a man's equilibrium, Miss Bliss. You make a man want to do all sorts of things he's never done before.''

"Like what?" she challenged.

"Like swim naked," he said. "I never did that before."

"Then it was high time you did."

"Did you?" His voice was suddenly serious. "Did you with somebody else?"

"With a lot of somebody elses," Rebecca said with a grin. "I was sixteen years old and I was spending the weekend at my girlfriend's parents' cottage in Canada. Five of us, all girls, went skinny-dipping. All we had on were these terrible white bathing caps. We swam and giggled and we came out of the water, trying to cover ourselves, and suddenly a flashbulb went off. It was my girlfriend's father, taking a picture."

"I'd love to see it," he said wickedly.

"So would I. But my friend, Dottie, was so furious she snatched the camera away from her dad, ripped the film out and burned it in the wood stove in the kitchen." Rebecca took hold of his ears and brought his face down to hers. "And that's the one and only time I ever swam in the nude until tonight with you."

He didn't know why it should make a difference, but it did because he wanted it to be a first for both of them. And he found himself thinking that he wanted to have a lot of firsts with Rebecca. That was what it would be, too, even with things that he had done before. Going to a football game would be new if she were with him. Hearing a symphony with her beside him, holding her hand when the music soared. That would be new. Sharing Christmas dinner with her at one end of the table and he at the other, Melinda between them, reaching for their hands when he said the blessing.

He didn't know how this magic between them had happened. He only knew that he couldn't bear the thought of parting with Rebecca, not after what they had shared.

That night, with the light of the moon shining down on them, they made slow and gentle love. Before he had taken her fiercely, hungrily, and she had responded with a hunger to match his. But this time was different. This time he touched her with such tenderness, such caring that she felt tears sting her eyes. And she responded in kind, holding him as he held her, whispering his name in that final moment, her voice breaking with an emotion that was so new that she didn't know what to call it.

Again, as she had before, when he made as though to move away, she said, "No, stay, Tom. Stay with me like this."

They slept and then woke to love again. How many times in that perfect moonlit night? Four times? Five? It didn't matter. The loving was slow, drowsy, perfect. And she knew that never again would there be a night like this. Never again would she feel the totality of being one with another person.

She awoke in that first faint light of morning while Tom still slept and eased herself away from him. Reaching for her T-shirt and panties, she pulled them on and went down to the shore. The sky in the east was gray with threatening clouds, and there was the smell of rain in the air. But it didn't matter. She was a beach person, always had been, always would be. In sun or fog or wind and rain, it didn't matter, she loved the beach because it was the perfect place to sort things out when life got complicated.

And this morning life was complicated. She needed time away from Tom to think about her feelings, her most complicated, unexplainable feelings.

For the first time in her life she had experienced a complete oneness with another person. It wasn't just sex, although making love with Tom was a mind-boggling, shattering, all-the-way-to-heaven experience.

Making love. She and Tom made *love* together. Was that the difference? The thought sobered her because she knew it couldn't last. When this was over, they would leave each other.

If things were different . . . if *they* weren't such different people perhaps there would have been a chance for them. But they were who they were. He was a Midwestern college professor; she was a government agent. And never the twain could meet.

"Damn it," she said aloud, and headed down the beach, careful to mark the place where they had camped.

Gulls floated over the sea, and frigate birds with their X-ray eyes swooped straight down after any fish that swam too close to the surface. She came upon a jellyfish that had been washed up onto the beach. It lay transparent blue in the pale light of day, its tentacles outspread, beached, helpless. She hunted for a stick, and when she found one, she carefully lifted the stranded creature and deposited him back in the sea.

Time passed; it was lighter now. She had to go back, because when Tom awakened he'd be worried about her. She'd wanted to do some serious thinking, to find answers, but she hadn't, not really. Her mind had skittered and scattered like the sandpipers that ran up and down the beach. All she could think about now was getting back to Tom. And perhaps, she thought with a smile, that was all she needed to know for right now. She'd awaken him with a kiss, they'd eat their last can of baked beans and some mangos, and maybe, just maybe, they'd make love again.

There was a curve in the beach just ahead. She decided she would go that far to see what was on the other side before she started back. Humming to herself, thinking about Tom, she rounded the curve of the beach. And stopped.

A soldier in a blue uniform, coffee cup halfway to his lips, stared at her, open-mouthed, too surprised for a moment to cry out.

Rebecca stared back, horrified. She saw other men, eight or ten of them, gathered around a campfire.

A shout went up. "The woman! It's the woman!"

She turned and ran for the trees.

"Get her!"

"Don't let her get away!"

Bare feet slipping in the sand, heart pounding in her chest, she ran toward the thickness of jungle trees. If she could reach them, she had a chance. She . . .

A hand on her shoulder spun her around. She knocked it away. Another man grabbed her and threw her down onto the sand. She kicked sand in his face and tried to squirm away. But the others came. They stood over her, a circle of them in their blue uniforms.

"It's the American," one of them said. "The woman General Feliciano has sent us to find."

Chapter 9

Without opening his eyes Tom reached out for her. She wasn't there. He came fully awake and called, "Rebecca? Rebecca, are you there?" But there was no answer.

He got up and went down through the trees toward the beach. The water was calm and in the distance he could see the white sails of fishing boats. But there was no sign of Rebecca. He was all alone on this great expanse of beach.

Had she gone swimming while he slept? With the thought that she might have ventured into the sea alone a knot of fear formed in his belly, for while the sea was calm there was always the danger of an undertow. What if she'd gotten caught in it? What if...? He shook his head. No, Rebecca was a strong swimmer. She'd have known what to do.

But the knot of fear grew.

He went back to where they had spent the night. The shorts she had worn yesterday were there, so were her sandals. He searched the trees nearby for some sign of her. There was nothing. He called her name and heard only silence. Even the birds were still.

He told himself that perhaps she had gone ahead to reconnoiter, to make sure of the direction they would follow today. He even managed to work up the semblance of anger to replace his growing fear. She should have awakened him. Damn it, why hadn't she?

Thirty minutes went by. He told himself he'd wait another fifteen before he went looking for her. He waited, but she didn't come.

Alarmed, the knot of fear growing with every minute, he took everything out of one of the backpacks and put it into the other. His face was grim, his mouth tight with strain. He looked around the place where they had spent the night and thought how it had been, how again and again they had made love, and how each time she had whispered his name in that final gasp of passion.

He went down to the beach and headed in the direction they had planned to take today, because if she had gone ahead, for whatever reason, that was the way she would have gone. He looked for footprints in the sand and told himself when there weren't any that if she had walked close to shore the waves would have washed them away.

Lost footprints. A chill of foreboding ran down his spine.

He went on. Ten minutes later he spotted her footprints higher up from the waterline, away from the shore. He quickened his pace, wondering as he did why she had gone so far.

He'd been gone for almost forty minutes when he saw the bend in the beach ahead, and his heart began to race because surely he would see her there, just around the curve of the beach. He'd give her hell. What are you trying to do? he'd yell at her. Scare me to death? Why didn't you wake me? Why didn't you tell me you were going on ahead?

His anger built, righteous anger at being left behind and because she'd been thoughtless. He'd tell her that. Tell her... He rounded the bend and his heart sank. There was no sign of Rebecca, nothing except that solitary stretch of beach and...he saw the other footprints. A lot of them. Heavy boot prints. Her bare footprints among the boot prints.

He ran forward, staggering in the sand as though he were drunk. His palms were sweating; he wiped them on the khaki shorts.

He found the place on the beach where men had camped, saw cigarette butts, part of a sandwich, empty cans of beer. With a cry of anguish he sank into the sand, his head in his hands because he knew now that they had found Rebecca. They had taken her.

"Where is he? Where is the American spy?"

"I don't know. He left me two days ago."

The same questions asked over and over again. The same answers. "I don't know where he is."

A short, squat corporal with a three-day growth of beard and tobacco-stained teeth cuffed her across the side of her head. "Tell me!" he shouted.

But her answer was always the same: "I don't know. He left me. I don't know where he is."

They mustn't capture Tom. He had to get away. She would do anything she could to keep them from finding Tom because if they captured him they would kill him. She wouldn't let that happen.

One of the soldiers, a skinny fellow in his early twenties, said, "Let me have her, Corporal Mendez. By the time I am through with her, she'll be only too happy to tell you whatever you want to know." He leered at Rebecca. "And *she'll* know what it's like to have a real man."

"Get away from her Valdez or I'll shoot off that thing between your legs that you're so proud of," the corporal said.

"Do you want her for yourself?" the skinny one asked. "If that's it, then you take her first, so long as you give each of us a chance at her."

The corporal's eyes narrowed. "And would you like me to tell General Feliciano that you and the rest of us have taken something that belongs to him?"

The young man's face went white under his tan. "I...I was only joking," he stammered. "I didn't mean—"

"You damn well had better not. A man lays a finger on the woman and I'll cut it off. She goes back to the general exactly the way we have found her. Is that clear?"

The others nodded, subdued, frightened by the ferocity of the corporal's voice.

They tied her hands behind her back, and two of them were left to guard her while the others spread out to search for Tom.

Stay where you are, Tom, she prayed. Please stay where you are.

In a little while the men who had been searching came back. "It's no use," they said. "Perhaps she's telling the truth. There's no trace of him. Only her footprints in the sand."

The corporal swore under his breath. "Let's go."

One of them grabbed her upper arm and propelled her ahead of him into the trees. The others followed, beating their way through the growth of jungle. They went on that way for three hours before they stopped to rest. When they did, they untied her hands and gave her water from one of the canteens and a piece of fruit. She was thirsty, and though she wasn't hungry, she ate the fruit because she knew she needed her strength. The minute they turned their backs she planned to make a break for it.

But they didn't turn their backs. They marched all that long day. Rebecca's legs hurt and her shoulders ached from being pulled back and tied. Mosquitoes buzzed around her face, but all she could do was shake her head and try to shoo them away.

At last when it began to get dark they stopped. She sank to the ground, too tired to speak. One of them started a fire and put a pot of water on to heat. When it was done, the corporal gave the nod to untie her. They gave her a tin cup of the coffee and a piece of hard bread.

The corporal said, "Tomorrow we'll reach the general's camp and I'll get a promotion for being the one to find the woman. That's what Feliciano promised. That and a substantial reward." He laughed and turned to Rebecca. "You'll make me a rich man, *señorita*."

"I have to go to the bathroom."

"What?" He scowled. "That's impossible."

"But, Corporal," an older man said, "if she has to go—"

"Then you take her, Barbosa. But guard her well. If she escapes, I'll kill you."

"She won't escape." The man Barbosa yanked her up off the ground. "This way."

"You'll have to untie my hands."

"I'm well aware of that, *señorita.*" He shoved Rebecca ahead of him into the thickness of trees, and when they reached a place a little distance from the others, he stopped. "Here," he said, and untied her.

Rebecca waited. He didn't move. "Please," she said. "Turn your back."

"I can't do that."

She lifted her chin. "You must." And when he didn't move, she said, "Surely, sir, you have a wife, sisters, daughters. Would you want them to suffer such an indignity?"

"No, but..." He hesitated while Rebecca held her breath. "Very well," he said at last. "But don't try anything."

He turned his back. She did what she had to do, all the while frantically searching for a stick, a stone, something. Her hand closed around the rough surface of a coconut. It wasn't what she wanted, but it would have to do.

"Hurry up," he said.

"All right. Give me a minute, please," she said, doing her best to sound frightened and meek. She came up slowly, stealthily, holding her breath lest she make a sound as she crept forward and raised the coconut over her head.

Something warned him, an instinct, a sound. He turned. "What...?"

She brought the coconut down hard just as he jerked to the left, and managed to strike him a glancing blow on the side of his head. He staggered back, momentarily stunned. *"¡Bruja!"* he yelled, and made a grab at her.

With the flat of her hand Rebecca chopped at the side of his neck. Stunned and enraged, he cried out. She turned and started running through the brush. He came after her, calling out in his fury, "She's getting away!"

Rebecca tore at branches and hanging vines, desperate in her struggle for freedom. Barbosa was close behind. He grabbed her shoulder. She pulled away, but he reached for her hair, fingers tightening, spread against her scalp. She cried out in pain and turned to strike out at him. But he wouldn't let her go. She clawed at him with her free hand and kicked out with her bare feet. He yanked hard on her hair. In pain she tried for a karate chop to his midsection. He dodged the chop and hit her a stunning blow to her face. She brought her left arm up to try to shield herself and with the flat of her palm smacked him a blow on one ear.

He staggered back, screaming in pain, and cried out, "I will kill you, *puta!*"

He came at her, head down, fists doubled. He struck again and again, her head, arms, shoulders, anywhere he could reach. He was too strong for her. She tried to fight back but she'd been weakened by the trek through the jungle, by the lack of food.

"I'll kill you," he shouted at her. "Kill—"

Suddenly he was yanked away from her, and she fell to the ground, barely conscious.

"Fool!" Mendez cried. He stood over Barbosa. "Stupid *pendéjo!* I told you we must take her to the general unharmed. What were you trying to do, kill her?"

"She tried to get away from me," Barbosa said, defending himself. "I tried to be decent and the bitch tried to kill me."

"How am I going to explain that to Felicaino? Shall I tell him you weren't man enough to guard a woman?" The corporal looked down at her, saw the condition she was in and glared back at Barbosa. "I won't try to protect you," he snarled. "I'll tell him it was you who beat her, and if he decides to shoot you on the spot, I'll do nothing to help you."

He went to Rebecca and stood over her, feet apart, angry, threatening. "As for you, *señorita,*" he said to her, "I've tried to be decent. I haven't let my men touch you. I've given you food and water and you've repaid me by trying to escape." He glared down at her. "Now I won't be so kind." He turned to Valdez. "Tie her," he snapped. "She's your responsibility now. If she gives you any trouble, tie her legs, too. If we have to, we'll drag her through the jungle."

Valdez yanked her to her feet, tied her arms behind her back and shoved her ahead of him to where they had set up camp. Once there he pushed her down at the foot of a tree. "You give us any more trouble, woman, and I'll hurt you in places where it won't show. Is that clear?"

Rebecca turned her face away.

"Answer me!"

"Go to hell," she said.

He drew his boot back and kicked her. The breath whooshed out of her with a low moan of pain. She curled up, away from him. Blood trickled down her chin from where Barbosa had struck her. She hurt. Oh, God, she hurt.

The men sat around the campfire. The corporal lighted a cigarette. "I'll be glad when we turn her over to Feliciano. She's more trouble than she's worth."

They talked far into the night, smoking, passing around a bottle of rum, ignoring her. But at last, after they posted a guard, they lay down near the fire and went to sleep.

Rebecca lay listening to their snores. She knew now that she had to be very careful. When they started out, the corporal had only wanted to get her safely to Feliciano. But he was angry now, so angry he had turned her over to Valdez. And Valdez was a dangerous man. She didn't dare risk another escape attempt.

She shook as though she had a chill, but it wasn't the night air that chilled her; it was fear of what tomorrow would bring, tomorrow when they turned her over to Maximo Feliciano. She didn't know what he would do with her; she only knew he was a vengeful man, a cruel man. And, yes, peacock proud. She had tricked him into believing that she found him attractive, that she was ready and eager to go to his bed. She had drugged him and she had made a fool of him. He would never forgive her for that.

By now he would know that she was with SIS and that she had come to San Sebastian for the specific purpose of freeing Thornton and of finding the secret missile site. He'd be angry enough to kill her, but maybe, just maybe, he wouldn't. She was a representative of the United States. Perhaps he would hold her as a hostage. She remembered those terrible cells underneath the Presidencia, the filth and the stench, and her stomach recoiled at the idea that that was very likely where she would end up when the general was through with her.

When he was through with her. That frightened her even more than the prospect of death.

She thought of her father and knew that although they weren't close he would be devastated by her death. He would blame Alex Hayden. It would be the end of their friendship. She thought about her mother, too. She remembered the scent of her perfume, the softness of the furs around her face.

But most of all she thought about Tom, and even though she was afraid, there was a part of her that was triumphant because she had led the soldiers away from him, because he was safe. He knew the location of the rendezvous point, and with luck he would be there at the appointed time tonight.

Don't let him try to come after me, she prayed. Please let him realize how important it is to get the film out of San Sebastian. Please let him be safe.

She looked up through the trees at the stars. Perhaps even now he was on the ship, having that ice-cold martini they had talked about. He would insist that a rescue attempt be made to save her. If Ed Blakley was on the rescue boat, he would try. Once before Ed had saved her. She hoped he would this time, too.

She shifted, trying to ease the pain in her back and arms, and when at last she found a more comfortable position, she closed her eyes. She thought about Tom and how it had been with them, the way they had loved each other last night. And she tried to imagine that her head rested against his chest rather than on the hard, damp ground. Finally, with the vision of him behind her eyelids, and the thought of him in her heart, she slept.

He followed the trail they had hacked through vines and the cigarette butts ground out against the jungle floor. His earlier panic had been replaced by a cold, hard edge of determination. They had Rebecca. He had to get to her before they took her to Feliciano.

He had her gun and the rifle and bandolier he had taken away from the soldier. If there weren't too many of them, and if he found a good vantage point, he'd be able to take them.

And kill them if he had to.

He had only killed one living creature in his life, and afterward he had vowed he would never kill another.

The year he had turned fourteen his father had taken him deer hunting in northern Michigan. "You're old enough now," his father had told Tom. "You're coming along with me this year."

He'd been so excited he had hardly been able to sleep the week before they had left. He was a man, a hunter just like his father. He was going to get his first deer.

His dad bought him a rifle, a heavy red-and-black mackinaw and a hunter's cap. They drove to Cadillac, Michigan, with three other men, hunting buddies of his father's, and they stayed at another friend's farm. The next morning at daybreak they started out. It was cold. The ground was hard with hoarfrost and the air smelled crisp and clean. A covey of quail flew out of the trees ahead of them, a cast of hawks swooped low over the scuddy-gray sky.

He'd felt that this had to be the happiest day of his life.

They came to a clump of bushes and low-hanging trees. "You and me will stay here," his father said. And the other men went on.

An hour passed, two. His feet were cold and so were his ears. He pulled the flaps of his hunter's cap down to cover them. His father's cheeks were bright red.

Beyond them they heard the rustle of leaves. A buck nosed through a stand of oak trees. His father said, "He's all yours, boy."

He raised his rifle. Steady, he told himself. Steady.

"Now," his father whispered.

He fired, and the sound was like a thunderclap ringing across the dry, cold land.

His father thumped him across his back. "By God," he cried. "You got him!"

They ran toward the fallen animal. It lay beneath the oaks, amid the acorns and the fallen leaves of autumn, not dead, but dying, staring up at them with wide, wet eyes.

That was the last time Tom had gone hunting. He'd given the gun back to his father and he had vowed he would never kill another living thing.

Now, because of Rebecca, he might have to kill, not an animal, but a man. Men. And he knew he would do it, that he would do whatever he had to to keep her safe.

He stopped only to eat the rest of the crackers and to drink some water. They couldn't be too far ahead of him, two or three hours at the most he guessed.

He went on until it was too dark to see the trail before he stopped. He tried to sleep, and dozed fitfully, alert for every noise.

As soon as it was daylight, he went on. An hour later he found the place where they had camped for the night. There were coffee grounds on the earth. He stopped and touched them. They were still warm.

He looked around under the bushes, the trees, not sure what he was looking for. A trace of her, something to tell him she had been here. Then he found it— the clasp that had bound her hair. He picked it up and saw, caught in it, strands of her hair. He closed his fist around it.

"I'm coming," he said aloud. "Hold on, Rebecca. I'm coming."

Chapter 10

Rebecca had reached a point of exhaustion where she knew she couldn't go on. The blows she had suffered had taken their toll, and she hadn't had enough food or water. For the past day and a half she had walked barefoot over jungle terrain and her feet were bruised and cut. She knew if she fell Valdez would show her no mercy. Finally, almost fainting, she called out, "Corporal... Corporal, wait, please."

He turned back, frowning. "What is it?"

"I... I have to rest. For a few minutes. Please."

"There's no time to rest."

"But I..." Her knees gave way and she sank to the ground.

"Get up!" he said furiously. And when she didn't, he turned to Valdez and snapped, "She's in your charge. Get her up."

The younger man grasped her shoulder and yanked her to her feet. "Walk," he ordered. "Walk or I'll—"

"*¡Alto!*" a voice cried out. "Stop where you are."

The men froze.

"Don't move, any of you." A sentry stepped out of the bushes, Uzi at the ready. "Identify yourselves!" he shouted.

"Corporal Mendez," the leader said. "We're a detachment from Sergeant Guzman's platoon. I have a prisoner, the woman General Feliciano is looking for. Take me to him immediately."

Feliciano? He was here? Rebecca went cold. Without thinking she jerked around, all of her instincts crying out for her to break free, to run for her life.

Valdez tightened his grip on her arm. With a mocking laugh he said, "There's no escape for you, woman. Soon you'll be at the disposal of our fine General Maximo Feliciano." He pulled her back, away from the others as they started forward through the jungle. "I'm only sorry I haven't had a chance at you first," he whispered close to her ear. "I'm *mucho mas hombre,* much more of a man than he is. A week with me and I'd have you licking my boots."

"Let me go!"

He laughed and ran his hands across her breasts. Grabbing her roughly to him, he pressed his lips to hers and forced his tongue into her mouth.

She struggled against him, but when it did no good, she bit down as hard as she could and at the same time brought her knee up between his legs.

He let her go and reeled back, one hand over his mouth, the other between his legs. Howling in pain, he started for her, but before he could reach her two of the men grabbed him.

"Don't be a fool," one of them said. "The general will kill you if you touch her."

They grasped Rebecca's arms. "Behave yourself, *bruja*," one of them snarled, "or we'll let him have his way with you."

She had no choice. There was nothing she could do but let him drag her forward into the camp.

It lay in a clearing, a temporary headquarters for the search parties that would branch off into different parts of the territory. There were four or five tents and one larger tent set a little aside from the others. A soldier, rifle at the ready, stood guard at the opening. Other soldiers, like the one who had stopped them, patrolled at either end of the encampment.

There was a stir of excitement when the corporal led his men forward. Soldiers ran out of their tents, crying, "They have the woman!"

Corporal Mendez took her away from the two men who had her. "Come with me," he said, taking charge. "I myself will hand you over to General Feliciano."

Soldiers gawked at her. One of them shouted, "She looks much the worse for wear, Corporal. What have you done to her?"

Mendez gripped her upper arm and dug his fingers into her tender flesh, and she knew he, too, was afraid of Maximo Feliciano. And though she was afraid, she straightened her shoulders, determined he wouldn't see her cower. She might be tired and dirty, bruised and battered, but she hadn't given up. Tom would have alerted Ed Blakley. They'd send a team of men in to rescue her. She just had to stay alive until they came. Stay alive...

The flap of the big tent opened and Feliciano stepped out. His green uniform was pressed and spotless, his boots were polished. The ribbons and rows of medals on his chest glittered in the late-afternoon sun.

Corporal Mendez saluted. "I have a prisoner. My men and I captured her a day and a half ago on the beach near Punta Arenas."

Feliciano looked her up and down the way he would a prize animal. Eyes narrowed, stroking his mustache, he said, "Good afternoon, Miss Bliss." A smile played across his lips. "How fortuitous that we meet again, though I must say you look much different than the last time we met."

He took in the torn and dirty T-shirt, the scratched legs, the bruises and the bare feet. "The night you came to my apartments you were clean, perfumed, beautifully dressed and, I thought, ready for love." Before she could step back he gripped the back of her neck and brought her closer. "I've been waiting a long time to finish what we started that night, Rebecca, but now I must wait a bit longer. We must do something about your appearance. I'm a fastidious man. I want my women clean when I take them."

"You'll never take me," she said.

"You think not?" He laughed. "My dear lady, you know so little about me."

He let her go and turned his attention to Mendez. "You bring her to me half dead," he said, his voice low, threatening. "If you yourself have touched her, or allowed your men to touch her—"

"I haven't, General. I swear!"

"Someone has beaten her." He thrust her toward Mendez. "Look at her! Look at her bruises! You could have killed her."

"It wasn't me, General. I swear it wasn't me. Ask her. She'll tell you. She tried to escape and one of my men beat her before I could stop him."

"His name?"

"Barbosa, General."

Feliciano turned to the guard at his right. "Find the man Barbosa and arrest him."

Mendez wiped a trickle of sweat from his face.

"Where is Professor Thornton, the American she helped to escape?"

"He . . . he wasn't with her, General. We searched, but we couldn't find him."

"You searched?" The slash of an eyebrow rose. "For how long, Corporal? Over how wide an area?"

Mendez ran a finger around his shirt collar. "Thirty minutes at least. And over a . . . a wide area."

"How wide? One mile? Two? Three?" Feliciano's face was red with anger. "You incompetent fool!" he raged. "You let the man slip through your fingers and you've brought me the woman so abused by you and your men that she's of little use to me."

"But, General—"

"Get out of my sight before I kill you!" Feliciano shouted.

Mendez let her go. Rebecca's knees sagged, but she managed to keep herself from falling.

Feliciano looked at her. "So we've come full circle. You made a fool of me when you took my prisoner. Now you're my prisoner."

"I'm a citizen of the United States. I demand—"

"You *demand?*" He shook his head. "My country has no diplomatic relations with yours, Miss Bliss. Your country can't help you." He took a step toward her. "I've waited a long time for this moment, but now, thanks to that stupid corporal, the moment must be delayed."

He turned to the guard. "Give her a tent and post a guard in front of it. Bring her soap and water, something to eat, and find a uniform small enough to fit her. And see to it that she isn't disturbed until I send for her." He looked at Rebecca. "I *will* send for you. And when I do you *will* tell me where Professor Thornton is. You'll tell me everything I want to know."

"I'll tell you nothing."

"Yes you will. Believe me, you will." He grabbed her chin and lifted her face to his. "And you'll give me what you denied me before, Señorita Bliss. Make no mistake about that. I intend to keep you for as long as it pleases me. After that..." He shrugged. "Perhaps when I'm done with you I'll be good-hearted enough to give you to my men."

She tried with every ounce of her will not to let him see her fear. "You'll never get away with this," she told him. "My government—"

"Will do nothing," he cut in. "You're expendable, Señorita Bliss. Nothing can save you now."

He snapped his fingers. "Take her away," he said to the guard. "And guard her well. If anything happens to her, you're a dead man."

The man grasped her arm and led her toward one of the tents. "Find another place," he said to the three men who stood in front of it. He untied her hands and pushed her ahead of him through the flap opening.

She sank down on the cot and covered her eyes with her hands. She was alone with her fear. There was nothing she could do but wait.

The sentry almost saw him. He would have except that by a stroke of good luck Tom had caught the sun glinting off the rifle. He ducked, all of his senses aware, flat on the ground. He thought for a moment about taking the sentry from behind, but if he did the sentry's relief would find him and the camp would be alerted. He didn't want that. His only chance was to take the camp by surprise somehow.

Slowly, cautiously, Tom crept backward, away from the sentry. It took him over an hour to circle around and find a vantage point on the crest of a hill where he could see the camp. He lay on his belly there, looking down at the scene below.

Soldiers paced back and forth, rifles over their shoulders. Guards were posted at each end of the camp. There were smaller tents, five of them, one large one, probably for the officer in charge. It was obvious this had been set up as a seach headquarters. That was why they had brought Rebecca here. She was down there in one of those tents.

His jaw bunched with the effort it took him not to go charging down the hill. But he knew he couldn't, that this was the one time in his life when he had to think clearly. Rebecca was in terrible danger, but she was alive. He had to believe they wouldn't hurt her because they had to take her back to the city to Feliciano. He would make himself wait and watch until they did. Very likely they'd take only a small detachment of men. He had her gun and the rifle. If he was very careful and very good, he'd be able to take them.

All he had to do was wait and be patient until they left the camp.

He tightened his hand on the rifle. The waiting would be hard, but he would do it. He had to because Rebecca's life was at stake. He couldn't let them take her to the city where Feliciano waited.

Tom rubbed a hand across his face. Feliciano. The thought of them taking her to the man he hated above all other men sickened him. He remembered what the general had done to him; he knew what he would do to Rebecca. He would do whatever he had to to prevent that.

Darkness came. He rested his back against a tree. Below him campfires were lighted. He could hear the voices, see the glow of their cigarettes. There was no sign of Rebecca. But he knew she was down there, somewhere, waiting as he waited.

She awoke an hour after daylight. It was hot in the tent. The T-shirt clung to her damp body. She pushed her tangled hair back off her face and swung her legs off the cot. Her body ached and her feet were bruised and sore, but the debilitating fatigue of the day before had lessened and she could think clearly enough to know that she was in one hell of a jam.

There was a bucket of water and a bar of soap in the tent, khaki pants, a man's undershirt and a pair of sandals. She bathed and put the clothes on. The pants were too big for her so she cinched in the belt and rolled the legs up. The sandals almost fit.

A voice called "*Señorita?* Are you awake?" And when she answered and opened the tent flap, a guard handed her a plate of black beans and rice.

Moros y christianos, Cubans called them. She ate every bit of them and felt stronger when she finished, ready to face what lay ahead.

Half an hour later the guard came for her. "The general will see you now."

She went out into the sun. It was hot. She looked around. Straight ahead of her lay the jungle. To the right there was a hill, to the left a grassy plain. The jungle would be her best bet, she decided. If help didn't come soon, that was where she would head. As soon as it was dark, she would make a break for it.

"Come along," the guard said. "Hands behind your back. Quickly now!"

She took a deep breath. With shoulders up and chin high she let the guard bind her hands and lead her to Feliciano's tent.

He stood in front of it, waiting for her. He wore khaki shorts this morning. His legs were skinny and slightly bowed. He held a riding crop in his hand.

"Inside!" he snapped. He took a chair behind a makeshift desk. "Leave her," he said to the guard.

There were two stools in the tent, but he didn't ask her to sit down.

"You appear to be better this morning. At least you're clean. It's too bad you were mistreated on your way here. My men are ignorant brutes, as you'll see when I turn you over to them."

Rebecca's mouth tightened, but she didn't respond.

"Suppose we get down to business. I want to know where Professor Thornton is."

"I have no idea."

"Really?" He seemed almost amused. "I know now that you work for the Secret Intelligence Service of the

United States and that you came to San Sebastian for the express purpose of trying to free Thornton. To do that you had to get close to me." He got to his feet. Hands behind his back, he walked up and down the narrow confines of his tent. His dark eyes were narrowed in thought, thin lips pursed.

"It isn't often I let a woman make a fool of me," he said. "My second and third wives tried and met with unfortunate accidents. As did one of my mistresses, Michele St. Cloud. She was an actress, you know. A lovely creature." He shook his head. "But she displeased me and I poisoned her."

Rebecca swallowed hard, thinking about the beans and rice she'd eaten this morning.

"But of all the women I've known, Rebecca, you've disappointed me the most. Therefore it's only fitting that you suffer the most." He stood directly in front of her. "You led me to believe that you found me attractive," he said in a low and deadly voice. "Then you drugged me so that you could free my prisoner. By doing that you've endangered the national security of San Sebastian. Now—" he took a step closer "—unless you tell me where Professor Thornton is I'll kill you."

The words had been softly spoken, but she saw death in his eyes.

Brave it out, she told herself. He won't kill you right away. Stall for time. Tell him something, anything. "I told your men that the professor and I parted company three days ago," she said at last. "I lied."

"Ah." He gave a sigh of satisfaction. "Now we're getting somewhere. But tell me, why was he not with you when you were captured?"

"He was asleep, a mile or two down the beach."

"Why didn't my men find him?"

"They only searched close to where they found me. They didn't bother going back down the beach."

"*¡Estúpidos!*" He swore a string of Spanish obscenities and thwacked his riding crop against his leg. "There are other search parties out. They'll find him."

"I don't think so."

"Why not!" His face grew red. "Tell me! Why not?"

"There was a boat," she said. "It will have picked him up by now."

"Liar!" He had his hand on his gun. Rebecca didn't breathe, didn't back away.

He took a step toward her, then stopped. "Guard!" he shouted. When the man came forward, Feliciano said, "Bring Corporal Mendez to me. At once!" To Rebecca he said, "If the professor is still in San Sebastian, I'll find him, Señorita Bliss. And when I do—"

Mendez came in. His hand shook when he saluted. "You sent for me, General?"

"That's why you're here, isn't it?" Feliciano moved closer. "Yesterday I thought very seriously about killing you, Corporal. I still may, but I've decided to give you a second chance. You're to go back to the place where you found Señorita Bliss. I want you to look for Señor Thornton and I want you to find him. If you don't..." Each word was punctuated by a finger stabbed at Mendez's chest.

Sweat dripped down Mendez's face, but he was too afraid to wipe it away.

Feliciano went back to his desk. "Take six of the men here in camp in addition to the men in your squad. You're to leave at once."

Mendez started to turn away, but stopped when Feliciano said, "You do know what will happen to you if you return without him, don't you?"

All color drained out of the corporal's face. "Yes, General," he whispered.

"Very well." With a wave of his hand Feliciano dismissed the man. To Rebecca he said, "There are other squads still out looking for Thornton. Perhaps they've even found him by now, but if they haven't, Mendez will. It's amazing what good results you get when a man knows his life depends on it." He went around behind the makeshift desk and sat down. "Now let us proceed with the questioning."

It went on for almost three hours. He badgered, he threatened. He demanded that she confess to him that Tom, too, was a member of SIS and that he had come to San Sebastian for the sole purpose of looking for the missile site.

Rebecca's legs hurt and her back ached, but she wouldn't give him the satisfaction of asking if she could sit down. Every time she thought she couldn't stand it another minute she thought about the burns on Tom's chest. He had withstood Feliciano's questioning, so could she. That gave her the strength to stand there and take whatever the general gave out.

At last one of his men came in with an important message, and he shouted for the guard to take her back to her own tent. "But I'll see you later. Then we'll do more than talk."

When she was alone, she sank down on the cot, exhausted by her ordeal, knowing there was more to come. She tried to quell her fear, but she couldn't. It was there, cold and ugly, deep in the pit of her stomach. If help didn't come, Maximo Feliciano was going to kill her. She was thirty years old, and this was the end. This was all she was ever going to have. And suddenly, for the first time since she had gone to work for Alex Hayden, she questioned what she did. Was it worth it? she asked herself. Was the work she did worth giving her life for?

She would never marry, never have children... Funny, she'd never really thought about having children, but she thought about it now, thought how it would be to hold a little one in her arms, a child that was part of her and part of... Tears stung her eyes.

She thought of what she had shared with Tom, the joy and the fulfillment he had given her. Tom, she thought. Be safe, Tom, for both of us. Go back to that home of yours, to your daughter. Live life for both of us, my darling. Live.

He had seen them take her into the big tent this morning, and it had been all he could do not to go screaming like a madman down the hill to her. She had been wearing green army pants and a man's undershirt. Her hands had been bound behind her back. For a moment she'd paused and looked around. He knew her well enough by now to know that she'd been looking for an avenue of escape. She'd looked up the hill, almost at the spot where he'd been hiding, and he had gasped with a pain that was almost physical.

"Rebecca," he had whispered, needing to hear her name. "Rebecca."

He waited and watched. He counted twenty-one armed men. One against twenty-one.

A little while later a corporal went into the big tent. When he came out, he called to several men, then motioned to some of the guards who had been patrolling. There was an argument. He drew his gun. The men went into different tents, and when they came out they had backpacks strapped on. Fifteen minutes later they disappeared into the jungle.

There were eleven left.

Almost three hours after she was taken into the tent Rebecca came out, still bound, head down, shoulders slumped. He could almost feel her exhaustion when she went into the tent they had taken her from.

He waited. Two hours passed. A guard was summoned to the bigger tent. He was there for only a moment before he went to where Rebecca was. He brought her out. They were halfway to the other tent when the flap opened and a man came out. He was wearing khaki shorts. He... Tom gasped and went cold all over. Feliciano! My God, Feliciano!

The general grasped Rebecca's upper arm. She struggled to break free, stumbled and fell. He stood over her. She tried to get up, but her hands were bound behind her. He yanked her up by her hair and shoved her ahead of him into the tent.

There was ice in Tom's veins, a terrible dryness of mouth. He took great gulps of air and tried to quell the sickness that rose in his stomach. Impotent with rage, he doubled his hands into fists. He wanted to kill the man who had hurt her and knew that when the time came he would. It took every bit of his willpower to wait. He wanted to rush headlong down the hill and into the general's tent. By the time the other men had spotted him, he'd be in the tent and there would be one less general in San Sebastian.

But that wouldn't help Rebecca. There were still too many of them. They'd kill him and she'd still be a prisoner.

Think! he told himself. Think!

He wished he hadn't stopped smoking. He wanted a cigarette so bad he could taste it. To light up, have just one drag, one whiff of burning tobacco. One...he went still. Burn. A fire! He looked down on the dry grassland. If he could get to it, start a brushfire that would draw the men away from the camp, he might have a chance of getting Rebecca away from Feliciano.

But first he had to get down the hill without being seen.

Chapter 11

Feliciano shoved Rebecca ahead of him into the tent. When she tried to break away, he cuffed her hard enough to make her ears ring and threw her down onto the cot.

"You made me look like a fool in front of my own men when you drugged me," he said. "And you freed a political prisoner."

"Thornton wasn't a political prisoner. He's a historian. He came to San Sebastian to do historical research."

"What kind of a fool do you take me for?" He hooked a stool with his foot and dragged it over. "You're going to tell me the truth about who you are and who the professor really is. If you do, it will go much easier for you. If you don't…" He let the words hang in the air.

"You already know who I am," Rebecca said. "If you have any sense at all, you'll set me free."

"Set you free?" Feliciano laughed. "Why should I do that now that I have you? You owe me, Rebecca, and I intend to collect. I'll keep you with me until I tire of you. And who knows, by then you may learn to like what I do to you."

"Not on your best day, General."

His dark eyebrows drew together. He reached into his shirt pocket for a cigar, bit the end off and lighted it.

She stared at the cigar. A terrible sickness rose in her, and she wanted to strike out, to wound him as he had wounded Tom. He sucked on the cigar, and the glow of ash grew brighter. She could feel Tom's pain, could almost smell his flesh burning. And hated this man as she had never hated before.

Feliciano looked down at her. "It makes no difference whether you come to me willingly or not. After all, a woman is merely a tool for a man's pleasure. I take what I want."

She fought the sickness, the revulsion. "You're stronger than I am, but let me warn you. I'll put up a fight—"

"Which I'll win, because if I have to I'll call two of my men to hold you down."

"What kind of a man are you?" she whispered.

"A man who's determined to have you, one way or the other. Take your clothes off."

"Go to hell!"

"Then I'll take them off for you." Before she could move away he grasped the top of her shirt and ripped. She brought her hands up to pull it together, and when she did, he grasped her wrists and shoved her back onto the cot.

She struggled to free herself, twisting away from him, fighting for survival.

He grabbed the top of her pants and cursed as he tried to open the belt. He was on her, over her, holding her with his legs, sharp knees cutting into her hipbones as he struggled to open his shorts.

Straining with effort, Rebecca pulled one hand free and smashed her fist against his mouth. His head snapped back, and blood ran from a cut lip.

¡Bruja!" he cried. "I'll kill you. Kill—"

"General! General, come quickly. There's a fire!"

Feliciano stared down at Rebecca, fist clenched, obsidian eyes wild with rage.

"General! You must come quickly!"

He hesitated, fist still raised.

Rebecca held her breath.

With a muttered curse he rolled away from her and ran to open the tent flap, wiping away the blood with the back of his hand. "By God," he raged at the guard. "If this isn't important, I'll kill you."

"There's a fire." The guard pointed at the burning grass beyond the tents. "We have to stop it or it'll burn us out, the tents, the munitions."

Rebecca sat up and tried to pull her torn shirt around her. She could smell the smoke and see the flames through the open tent flap.

"Put it out!" Feliciano screamed.

"There's no water except what we have for drinking."

"Then use it. Use whatever you have. Take all the men. Hurry! Go!"

The guard turned and ran, shouting, "Every man to the fire! Quickly!"

Feliciano pulled the belt through the loops of his shorts and grasped her hands to bind her. "I'll be back," he threatened. "And when I return—"

"Let her go." Thornton moved into the tent. Without taking his eyes from Feliciano he asked Rebecca, "Are you all right?"

She stared at him, eyes wide with shock. "Tom! I thought you'd gone. What are you doing here? What…?" She tried to gather her wits. "Yes. I…I'm all right." She scrambled up off the cot.

"Take his gun. Tie him."

"How did you get here? I don't understand?" Even as she asked the questions she disentangled the belt from her wrists and ran toward Feliciano.

"Hurry!" Tom said. "We've got to get out of…" He saw her bruises and sucked his breath in. "My God," he whispered. "What have they done to you?"

"I'm all right," she said, and made the mistake of looking at him.

Feliciano grabbed her. He pulled a short, snub-nosed revolver from the holster at his side and pointed it at her head. "Back away or I'll kill her," he told Tom in a low, deadly voice. "Put the rifle down. That's it. Now drop the gun."

Tom looked at Rebecca. Her eyes were wide, her face strained, frozen. He had no choice; he knew if he didn't do as he was told Feliciano would shoot her.

"You started the fire, didn't you, Professor Thornton? It was a clever diversionary tactic to lure my men away from the camp, and by the looks of it, it well may burn us out." He pulled Rebecca closer, his arm across her chest. "You've caused me no end of trouble, you know. I think it's time I disposed of you."

"Let him go!" Rebecca cried. "I'll do anything you want. I won't fight you. I swear I won't—"

"How touching." His gaze met Thornton's. He brought the gun up and leveled it at Tom's heart. "Say *adiós,* Professor. Your time is up."

"No!" Rebecca cried. She grabbed Feliciano's wrist. He fired, but the shot went wild. He struck out at her, but she moved in closer. Her hand closed on the cold steel. He wrenched the gun away. She dug her nails into his hand and fought for the weapon.

Tom scooped up the gun he had dropped, but he couldn't shoot because Rebecca and the general were too close, locked in a life-and-death struggle, fighting for the gun. Feliciano was stronger, but she was very quick. He freed one hand and brought his doubled fist down hard against the side of her head. She cried out in pain, but like a small, fierce bulldog, hung on to the gun.

Inch by inch the general brought the gun up until the barrel was pressed against Rebecca's chest. She fought with him, struggling to turn it.

Tom raised his gun. He had to take the chance. He had to—

The shot rang out. And still Rebecca and the general were locked in their deadly embrace. Then his face changed, sagged, and slowly, like an accordion without a player, he folded and fell.

Rebecca stood where she was, still holding the gun, staring down at the man she had killed.

"Rebecca!"

She looked up at Tom.

"We've got to get out of here," he said.

She swallowed hard. "Yes." She shoved Feliciano's gun into the waistband of her pants.

Tom picked up the rifle. "We'll head for the jungle."

She looked down at the general, then away. She had killed a man. She . . . No, she wouldn't think about it now. There was no time.

Tom opened the tent flap and peered out. "They're all fighting the fire. We can make a break for it." He took her hand and squeezed it. "Come on."

They went cautiously out of the tent. From the direction of the fire they could hear voices, shouted orders. They ran past the line of tents toward the growth of jungle trees. They were almost there when suddenly behind them they heard a shout. *"¡Alto!"* a guard cried. "Stop!"

Bullets whizzed over their heads. They ducked low and kept running. Tom spun around, raised the rifle to his shoulder and fired at the man who was shooting at them. Then he turned and sprinted for the trees, Rebecca close behind him.

Another round was fired. Tom fired back. The lone guard fell. "Run!" he cried to Rebecca. But she was down on her knees. He grabbed her hand and pulled her to her feet, thinking she had stumbled, his only thought that they had to reach the trees before anybody else spotted them.

They ran on until they reached the cover of the jungle. "We made it," he panted. "We . . ." He saw the blood. "Oh, my God, you've been shot!"

"It's not bad. I can go on. We've got to get out of here. Got to keep moving."

He looked down at her leg. Her pants were torn where the bullet had struck her thigh on the outside, just below her hip. Blood was running down her leg. He took his shirt off, ripped a strip from the bottom and wrapped it around her leg. "Do you think you can walk?" he asked.

She nodded.

"Rebecca, I..." He touched her hair. "I wish it had been me."

"But then I might have had to carry you," she said, trying to make light of her wound. She put her arms around his waist, her head against his chest. "I don't know how you got here. I only know I've never been so glad to see anybody in my life." She looked up at him. "We've got to get going."

"I know." He kissed her and let her go.

There hadn't been any initial pain, but there was now. She tried to ignore it. They couldn't stop; they had to get away before the men fighting the fire came back. They'd discover the guard and find Feliciano. Feliciano. She had never killed a man before. She hated it that she had, but knew she would do it again if she had to. She'd do anything she had to protect Tom.

The thought of him kept her going in spite of the pain. She knew their lives depended on her being able to keep going.

In a little while Tom said, "We can stop now. You've got to rest."

She didn't need any urging. She took a sip of the water he gave her, leaned back against the trunk of a tree and closed her eyes. Her face had a grayish cast. Her upper lip was beaded with sweat.

He knelt beside her. "Better let me have a look at that leg."

He ripped part of the pant leg open. Blood had soaked through the bandage. He tore another strip off his shirt and rebandaged her. She needed a doctor, but he had no idea where they could find one in this god-forsaken land. Even if they could, it would be dangerous. As soon as the soldiers came back from fighting the fire and found that their general had been killed, they'd come after them. He had to find a place where they'd be safe, where he could take care of Rebecca's wound.

"Drink some more water," he said.

She opened her eyes. "I thought you'd gone, Tom. I thought you'd go to the rendezvous point to wait for the boat."

"I would never have left without you, Rebecca."

She touched the side of his face. "I wanted you to be safe."

He kissed the palm of her hand. "Not without you, Rebecca."

"Tom . . . ?" She shook her head. "We've got to go on."

"Yes." He helped her up, but instead of starting off again he put his arms around her and held her close. "I almost went crazy when you left me," he murmured against the fall of her hair.

"I didn't leave you, Tom. I just went for a walk on the beach, farther than I intended to because I was thinking about you, about us, about that night and how we . . ." A trace of color crept into her cheeks.

"How we'd made love all night?"

She rested her hands on his shoulders and looked up at him. "Yes, that's what I was thinking about. And I literally ran right into the soldiers. They grabbed me and then they searched for you. I told them we'd parted company a few days before."

He tightened his arms around her. "Today is the second time you've saved my life, Rebecca." A smile played around the corners of his mouth. "Isn't there a saying, a Chinese legend that says if you save a man's life you're forever responsible for his life?" He kissed her and said, "You may never get rid of me, Rebecca."

"Tom, I—"

He cut her off. "We've got to go on. We've got to get that bullet out as soon as we can."

With what? she wondered. A penknife to cut with, a bullet to bite on? But she said nothing as she followed Tom through the jungle.

The heat was oppressive, the humidity so high that it seemed as though there wasn't enough air. She tried to think about things that were cool: vanilla ice cream, watermelon, baked Alaska. Not about the pain in her leg. Think about ice tinkling in a glass of iced tea, she told herself. Lemonade...

Everything got hazy. She thought it was just the heat rising off the jungle floor, and when she staggered, she made herself believe the ground was uneven.

"Are you all right?" Tom asked.

"Sure," she said. "Sure."

"They're going to be searching the jungle and the beach area," he told her. "We'd better head into the mountains, up toward the volcano."

Up. They were going up. She couldn't even walk a straight line and they were going up.

He put his arm around her to help her, concern and worry written on his face. Again and again he asked, "Are you all right, Rebecca? Can you make it?"

And finally she knew she couldn't. Her legs wouldn't go anymore. She slumped to the ground and rested her head on her knees. "Sorry," she managed to say. "'Fraid I can't go any farther. Not for a while."

"It's all right. We'll rest here."

They were high into the mountains. In the last light of day he could see the volcano, and in the distance the glow of campfires. There was a village up there, maybe a doctor. He'd have to take a chance that the people who lived there were so far removed from the city they wouldn't have heard about his escape or Rebecca. But even if they had, even if there were police there, or soldiers, he had to get help for her. That was what mattered now.

He let her rest for a few minutes, then he picked her up in his arms.

"I can walk," she protested weakly.

"No, you can't." He kissed her cheek. "It's going to be all right. We're going to make it, Rebecca."

Almost thirty minutes had gone by when he heard the sound of a church bell—solemn, sonorous, calling the faithful to evening prayer.

"We've reached a village," he said. But Rebecca didn't answer.

He leaned his face toward hers. She was burning with fever.

Frantic and afraid, with the raw edge of panic tightening his gut, he pressed on. He knew she was bleeding, knew that life was seeping out of her body. He had to get help. He had to.

With the breath coming hard in his chest Tom pushed his way through a thickness of tangled vines. The sound of the bells was closer. He could smell woodsmoke. He went on. It couldn't be much farther. He had to get to the village. Had to... And then he saw it—a scattering of houses, a church, a school, the village square.

There were people in the square. Others were coming from the church. They stopped and stared at him. Someone called out and a priest came out of the church. For a moment no one spoke, then the priest came down from the church steps and asked in Spanish, "The woman is hurt?"

"Yes, Father. She needs help. A doctor."

"I see." The priest, a tall, almost painfully thin man in his late seventies, laid a bony finger alongside his nose. "We have no doctor in our village, but we will do what we can to help you, my son." He motioned to one of the women in the group that had come closer. "Maria," he said, "the *señora* has been injured and needs help. Will you take her into your home?"

"Sí, Padre. ¿Cómo no?"

She was a dark woman, short and squat. Her hair hung in neat braids down her back. Her skin was the color of chestnuts, and as dry. Her eyes were so brown they were almost black and her nose was eagle-like.

"Maria is a descendant of the Carib Indians," the priest said. "She is a *curandero,* a healer, a good woman. You and your wife can stay with her, Señor...?"

"My name is Thomas."

"Señor Thomas." He rested a hand on Tom's shoulder. "I am Father Valverde. Go with Maria. She will give you food and shelter and she will do what she can for your wife."

His wife. That gave him a strange feeling in the pit of his stomach. He knew he should have corrected the priest, but it seemed easier to go along with the assumption that Rebecca was his wife. But that wasn't the only reason: it made him feel somehow closer to her.

He followed Maria to a small wooden house at the end of the street. Two pigs lay in the dirt at the side of the house, and a goat was tied near the steps.

"*Pase,*" she said. "Come in."

The house was almost bare. The dirt floor was partially covered with straw mats. There were two chairs, a table and an open cupboard with a few dishes. Pots and pans hung in the fireplace. The woman lighted a kerosene lamp. Then she gestured for Tom to follow, opened a door at the far end of the room and motioned to the bed. She pulled back the blanket. The sheet beneath it was clean.

Tom eased Rebecca onto the bed. "I'll need hot water," he said to the woman. "Soap and a knife. Something for a bandage."

He raised Rebecca's head and held the water bottle to her lips. "Rebecca? Honey?"

Her eyelids fluttered. "Where are we?"

"We're in a village."

"Leg hurts."

"I know, baby." He put a pillow that felt as though it had been stuffed with acorns under her head. "A very nice lady has taken us in, Rebecca. She's a nurse. She'll know what to do."

A nurse? That was stretching the truth. The priest had said the woman was a healer, but Tom knew enough Spanish to know that the word *curandero*, literally translated, meant witch doctor. He was grateful for Maria's hospitality, but he didn't want her touching Rebecca.

By the time he'd stripped off Rebecca's clothes and helped her into the plain cotton nightgown Maria had given him, she had returned with a chipped pan of hot water, a bar of brown soap, a knife and a cup of tea. "It is an herb tea," she said. "It will help."

Tom hesitated, then held the cup to Rebecca's lips. "A special blend," he told her, forcing a smile.

Rebecca took a few sips and lay back against the pillow. "Tastes awful."

"That means it's good for you." He unwrapped the bandage from her leg. The wound was red and swollen and caked with blood. "I'm going to have to take the bullet out," he said gently.

"You know how?"

He wanted to lie, wanted to say he'd done this before, but he couldn't. He shook his head. "I took a refresher first-aid course a month before I came to San Sebastian. There was a section on wounds." He rested a hand on her shoulder. "I'll do my best, Rebecca, but it's going to hurt like hell."

"A doctor made the mistake once of squeezing my infected toe and asking if it hurt. I socked him." She managed a smile. "Watch yourself, Doc. I've got strange reflexes."

Some of his tension eased. "I'll remember that," he said.

He asked for another pan of hot water so that he could wash his hands. Then he cleaned the wound and picked up the knife. "I'm going to start now."

Rebecca closed her eyes. She flinched when she felt the knife cut into her flesh, but tried not to move. Her forehead was beaded with sweat; her teeth were clenched.

Tom worked without speaking. He probed cautiously, felt the knife hit steel. "I'm getting it," he said under his breath. "Hold on."

The woman lifted the lamp higher. He got the knife under the bullet and reached in with his fingers. Rebecca tried to hold back a moan of pain, and failed.

"Got it," he said.

But she had fainted.

"It is better that she did," Maria said. She handed him white strips she had torn from a sheet. He folded a pressure pack against the wound, then bound it.

When that was done, he covered Rebecca with a blanket and bathed her face with cool water. She opened her eyes.

"Finished?" she asked weakly.

"It's all done," he said. "All you have to do now is rest."

Maria handed him the tea. "Your wife must drink this. It will help."

He put a hand under Rebecca's shoulders and raised her head.

"Wife?" she asked.

"Wife," he said, and kissed her forehead. "Now drink your tea."

Chapter 12

Rebecca slept fitfully and dreamed unpleasant fearful dreams. She saw her mother and cried, "Mama, Mama." Then, weeping with joy, she reached out her arms, longing for an embrace, the touch of fur against her cheek and the remembered scent of her mother's perfume. But before she could reach her, her mother disappeared and it was Feliciano who stood there, his arm raised, threatening, dangerous. Her skin tightened and her breath came in short, panting gasps. He had a gun, but it wasn't like any gun she had ever seen. The barrel was too long, and curved so that it was pointing at him rather than at her. She heard the frightful explosion and saw the bloody wound in his chest. And she watched, horrified, as the blood spread and grew. He looked down at it and said, "You've killed me."

"No!" she cried. "No, it wasn't me! It wasn't me!"

"Shh," a voice said. A hand soothed her forehead. "Go back to sleep," he said, and she did.

Tom looked down at her, wondering what nightmares haunted her sleep, what bitter experiences she had had before she had come to San Sebastian. She had told him about Caracas, but had there been other times like that, other places, other countries where her life had been in jeopardy?

Why did she do it? he wondered. What was there inside her that drove her to do such dangerous work? He wished he knew.

He brought one of the chairs from the other room and sat beside her all that long night, holding her hand, soothing her when she cried out.

Over and over in his mind he relived the events of the day—the crackle of flames when he started the fire, the cry of soldiers sounding the alert, deserting their posts to put it out. Knowing deep in his soul that when they had gone he would kill Maximo Feliciano. Instead the general had almost killed him, and he would have if it hadn't been for Rebecca. Rebecca who had struggled for the gun. Rebecca who had killed for him.

He thought of their desperate flight toward the safety of the jungle, the shots ringing out. Rebecca falling wounded. He thought of her courage and her bravery, and of his own desperate attempt to get her safely away to somewhere where she could get medical attention.

Some medical attention—an old woman who was the village witch doctor and a professor who'd had a course in first aid.

He felt her forehead. She burned with fever. He bathed her face and her hands in cool water, and prayed as he had never prayed before. Toward morning he fell asleep, his head on the bed so that he could touch her. Once he felt her hand soothing the top of his head, but when he rose he saw that she slept.

By morning Rebecca's fever was worse. She was restless, in pain, mumbling incoherently. He held her head and helped her to drink a little of the tea Maria had brought.

"I will make a poultice," the Indian woman said. "Sometimes it works, sometimes not. Your wife is very ill, *señor.* It would be best to prepare yourself for the will of God." Before he could answer she went out.

Prepare himself! No, by God, no! He wasn't going to let her die. He'd get her back to the city where he could find a doctor for her. He'd do anything, turn himself into the police, the army. Let them shoot him. It didn't matter. Nothing mattered except that she get help, that she live.

The priest came. "Is there a vehicle in the village?" Tom asked. "Is there any way I can get her to the city?"

"No, my son. There is nothing. We are a remote village, and poor. We have a few donkeys that our men use for plowing the fields. Nothing more." He looked down at Rebecca. "All that we can do now, Señor Thomas, is pray."

He came back later that afternoon. "There is no change?" he asked.

"No, Father." Tom ran a distracted hand through his hair. He hadn't slept. His eyes were bloodshot. There were lines in his face that hadn't been there before. "I don't know what to do."

Father Valverde looked down at Rebecca. "Is your wife Catholic?"

Tom hesitated. He couldn't say that he didn't know, that he had no idea what his wife's religion was because she wasn't his wife.

"Yes," he said. "She's Catholic."

Father Valverde put a purple stole around his neck and anointed Rebecca's forehead with a small flask of oil from his robe.

Tom looked on. He watched the priest's lips move in prayer. He looked at Rebecca's still, pale face. He wanted to cry out, Why are you doing this? She isn't dying. You're wrong. You're wrong! But he said nothing. He only gripped the end of the bed and held on until his knuckles turned white.

When the priest finished, he put a hand on Tom's shoulder. "I will pray for her."

Maria came in to change the poultice. The wound was still red and swollen. She sighed and shook her head. "We shall see," she said, and left the room.

Rebecca's fever rose. Tom bathed her face, chest and arms. By evening chills racked her body. He asked Maria for another blanket. "I have only the one blanket, *señor,*" she said.

He sat on the edge of the bed and tried to hold Rebecca, to warm her, but nothing helped. He knew that somehow he had to stop the chills. She couldn't go on this way. God, he felt so helpless. If only there was a way... Suddenly he began tearing at his clothes. Then, naked, he pulled back the blanket, got into the bed beside her and gathered her into his arms. Her eyes opened and she put her face against his neck.

"You have to fight, Rebecca," he said. "Fight, my love." He held her close, warming her with his body heat, and over and over again he said, "Fight, Rebecca. Fight."

And finally, after an eternity of time, the terrible shaking subsided and she slept.

He held her all through that long night, held her with a tenderness he had felt only for his child. He touched the fragile bones of her spine, the gracefully delicate neck. He kissed her feverish forehead, and though he knew she couldn't hear, he said, "Live, Rebecca. Live for me."

At last, still holding her close to him, he slept.

He awoke once in the night to find that her fever had broken and that her body was wet with perspiration. He got up and helped her to a sitting position.

"Sleepy," she mumbled.

"I know, dear." He drew the damp nightgown over her head and dried her with a towel Maria had left in the room. "Go back to sleep now."

"With you."

"Yes, with me." He lay down beside her and drew her into his arms. She snugged her head into the hollow of his shoulder and slept. In a little while so did he, content at last with the knowledge that she was better.

Two days later Rebecca was sitting up in bed, wearing another of Maria's white cotton gowns, eating the soft-boiled eggs that Maria had prepared. She had slept almost all day yesterday, but this morning when she awakened she'd announced she was hungry. Her eyes were bright and there was color in her cheeks.

"Thank God for Maria's poultice," Tom said. "It helped get rid of the infection and made you well again."

Rebecca paused with the spoon halfway to her mouth. "No, it was you, Tom. It was you who made the difference. You saved me with your warmth and with your caring.''

He took a deep, shaking breath. ''And I do care, Rebecca. I care very much.''

She touched the side of the bed, and when he sat beside her, she said, ''Dear Tom, I came to San Sebastian to rescue you, but you're the one who's taken care of me.''

''You saved my life. You killed a man for me.''

A shadow passed over her face, and she lowered her eyes. ''I hate that I did,'' she whispered. Then, looking into his eyes, she said, ''But I'd do it again if I had to. I'd kill anyone who tried to hurt you.''

''I know what it cost you.''

For a moment she didn't answer. Then she asked, ''Do you think we're safe here? Will any of these people report us to the authorities?''

''I don't think we're within miles of any kind of authority. But even if we were, Rebecca, I honestly don't believe these people would say anything.''

''But we can't stay here, Tom. We have to leave.''

''We're going to stay here until your leg has healed. Until you're well again.''

''But—''

He put a finger against her lips. ''You've been through a lot these past few days, Rebecca. You need to rest.''

''But the boat, Tom.''

''You said if we didn't make the first rendezvous it would return.''

''It will, for a while.''

''Then we'll just have to take our chances.'' His voice firmed. ''You can't go trekking through the jungle again, not with your bad leg, not for a while at least." He rested his hands on her shoulders. "I'm not going to take a chance with your life, Rebecca."

"But the soldiers might find us. What if they come to this village? What if—"

"I don't think they will, but if they do, I believe Father Valverde will protect us."

"Father Valverde, the village priest." She tried to remember. "He was here, wasn't he? I remember him praying, doing something..."

"He came two days ago. Because he thinks we're man and wife he asked me if you were a Catholic, and I..." He lifted his shoulders. "I didn't know, but I told him you were. He wanted to give you...to give you..." He shook his head, unable to go on.

Rebecca reached for his hand. "They used to be called the last rites, Extreme Unction. Now it's the anointing of the sick." She tightened her hand on his. "Was I that sick?"

Tom leaned his head against her breast and said, "Yes, Rebecca. I was afraid. I—"

"Shh," she said. "It's all right, Tom. I'm all right now." She stroked his hair, and the suggestion of a smile played across her lips. "You told him I was your wife?"

He raised his head and looked at her. "He assumed we were and I..."

"You didn't bother to correct him."

"No."

Something clutched at her insides and made her wonder what it would be like to be married to Tom. To be Mrs. Thomas Thornton. The thought gave her a fluttery feeling in the pit of her stomach, and she decided she wouldn't think about it, not for a while at least.

When this was over...when—not if—they got safely out of San Sebastian, they would of necessity go their separate ways. She had her life, and an unstable life it was. In another month or two she'd have an assignment that would take her only God knew where, to Europe, the Middle East, to any number of different countries. And Professor Tom Thornton would go back to his life and his child in Brookfield Falls, Illinois. It was a life she could never be a part of.

But for now... She stroked his hair, and in a little while, because she was very tired, she drifted back to sleep.

By the end of the week, Rebecca was able to venture out of the house. She said she would like to see the village, and Tom held her arm as they walked to the square. When they came to the church, she asked, "Would you mind?" And together they walked up the steps and into the coolness of the sanctuary.

It was a poor church, and plain. There were no stained glass windows. No cherubims or seraphims looked down from the dome. No saints adorned the altar, only a simple cross and a rough-hewn figure of Christ.

They sat in one of the pews, and when she knelt, Tom came down beside her.

I know so little about you, he thought. You came into my life so suddenly, so violently. You're not at all the kind of woman I ever thought I needed or wanted. You're different from anyone I've ever known. Different from me. And yet...

Her eyes were closed. Her face, half hidden by the fall of her freshly washed hair, was solemn, serious. Her pale hands were clasped in prayer. He covered them with his own. She opened her eyes and turned to look at him. Her gaze locked with his, and it was as though time stood still, for him and for her. He was one with her as he had never been with anyone before, here in this simple church in this remote village.

Her fingers curled around his. He heard her whisper his name, and suddenly it didn't matter that there were differences between them. She was the woman he wanted, the one person in the world he never wanted to be apart from.

"I love you," he said.

Tears, like drops of crystal rain, rose from the depths of her green eyes. She leaned her face against his hand. He felt her tears and raised her face so that she could look at him.

"It's so soon," she whispered.

"I know." He waited, scarcely daring to breathe.

"Me, too," she said.

"Me, too, what?"

She wiped the tears away. "I love you, too."

They lay together that night, as they had every night since she'd been hurt. The other nights he had only held her, content to be close, to soothe her when the bad dreams came. But this night it was different.

She brought his head down to rest on her breast, and with a sigh he turned her so that he could kiss her there. They lay like that, eyes closed, content for a little while with this small touching. He feathered tender kisses against her skin as he moved closer and ever closer to the poised and ready peak. He closed his teeth around it, to taste and tease and gently scrape.

When she moaned low in her throat, his passion grew. He whispered her name against her breast, and felt her response in the yearning of her body toward his, in the quick little puffs of breath, the slow catlike stretch of her limbs.

He knew how good it was going to be for them, but he made himself wait, as he made her wait. And when, after what seemed like an eternity of time, he came up to take Rebecca's mouth, she answered his kiss with an intensity that left him breathless.

"I'll be careful," he said. "I won't hurt you." He eased himself over her. "Is it all right? Am I too heavy? I'm not hurting you?"

She kissed the side of his face, pressed against the small of his back and urged, "Come into me now, Tom. Come into me, darling."

Tears stung his eyes because she loved him, and because she wanted this as much as he did. He kissed her again, and gently, carefully, joined his body to hers. Her warmth took him in, and it was like coming home. It was everything he had ever dreamed that love could be.

He moved against her, filling her. This is all of me, he wanted to tell her. All that I am, and I give it to you, Rebecca. My Rebecca.

She clung to him, her arms around his back, caressing his shoulders, lifting herself to him, giving of her body and of herself, whispering his name in a litany of pleasure. "Oh, Tom, darling . . . darling."

He moved against her, thrusting deep, then withdrawing to thrust again and again.

"Oh, please," she whispered.

"Now?" he asked. "Now?"

She didn't want it to end. She wanted it to go on and on, but, oh, she couldn't stand this sweet torture, this rapturous feeling that drove her on. She wanted more and still more. It was beyond comprehension, beyond anything she'd ever know.

He captured a breast. He caressed it with his tongue, and it was too much, too long past bearing. She cried out, unashamed, unrestrained, unable to hold back. And when she did, he took her mouth, crying out as she had cried, and together, heart against beating heart, they rose to the unbelievable heights of mutual passion.

When their breathing evened, he drew her down on his breast. He told her how lovely she was. And held her until she slept.

The following morning Father Valverde came to speak to Tom. "One of our village men came from the city yesterday," he said. "The country is in a turmoil. General Maximo Feliciano has been shot and killed. His soldiers are looking for the man and woman who killed him." The old priest looked at Tom. "An American man and woman."

"I—"

"No!" The priest held up his hand. "I do not want to hear. I do not like what General Feliciano did to my country, but I am a law-abiding man. The less I know the better."

"I think it would be best for my...my wife and I to leave as soon as possible."

"Yes, so do I. She is able to travel?"

Tom nodded.

"Where will you go?"

"To the coast. My wife is an agent of the United States government, Father. There was to have been a ship waiting for us, but too much time has passed. I don't think it will be there now. We'll have to find our own way, try to buy passage.''

''It will be dangerous. There are many who do not like our present form of government, but many who do. There are soldiers out searching. You do not know your way.'' The priest shook his head. ''Let me think about this. I will return later. Wait here until I do.''

''Father Valverde was here?'' Rebecca asked when Tom went into the room they shared. ''Was it anything special?''

He nodded. ''They know about us. We've got to leave.''

''I see.'' She looked around at this place that they had shared. It was a simple room, an ugly room, with only the bed and a stand for the basin they washed in. But yet... She gazed out the window that looked over fields of corn, mango trees and wildflowers. She had almost died in this room; she had found love here.

''I'll be sad to leave,'' she said, and put her arms around him.

He kissed the top of her head. ''Yes, so will I.''

''When must we go?''

''Today. Father Valverde told me to wait here. We'll leave as soon as he returns.''

There was little they could do by way of preparation. Tom bought two canteens and a few cans of food at the general store, as well as a man's shirt for Rebecca. He thought that with luck they could make the coast in a day and a half. Once there they would go to the rendezvous point in case the ship they were supposed to have met two weeks ago was still there. If it wasn't... No, he wouldn't think about that.

The priest came at dark. He had a young man with him. "This is Enrique García," he said. "He will take you to the coast."

"It's best we leave now," Garcia said. "The patrols won't venture into the jungle at night."

"Very well." Tom held out his hand to the priest. "There's no way we can ever thank you for your kindness. But believe me, Father, we do thank you."

"Go safely, my son." The old man rested a hand on Rebecca's shoulder. "And you, my daughter. Go with God."

"*Gracias,* Father." She turned then to Maria. "And thank you, Maria. Thank you for everything."

"*Por nada.*" The Indian woman handed her a paper sack filled with sandwiches. "I am sorry you did not like my tea."

"I may not have liked it, but I drank it because I knew that anything that tasted that bad had to be good for me." Rebecca smiled. "*Gracias, Maria. Gracias* for everything."

Tom slipped his arms into the backpack and picked up the rifle.

"I hope you will not have to use it," Father Valverde said.

"I hope not, either." Tom reached for Rebecca's hand. "Ready?" he asked.

"Ready," she said.

Chapter 13

"You're the Americans the soldiers are looking for?" Enrique García leaned back against the trunk of the tree and lighted a cigarette. The age of some of Tom's students, he was tall and dark, with Indian features and a short but solid body. "You're the one who killed General Feliciano?"

Tom looked at Rebecca. He tightened his hands around the rifle. "That's right."

"There's a ten-thousand-dollar reward for your capture." García studied the glowing end of his cigarette. "They should give it to you for killing Feliciano. Our elected president was an old man, but he was honest and he did his best. His only problem was that he was too good, too trusting. Feliciano was the son of his best friend, and when Feliciano's father died, President Aleman took him into his home and treated him as his son. He sent him to school in Spain. He did everything for him. And when he returned from Spain our president gave him a job in the army."

García spit through his teeth. "He rose through the ranks by stepping on his fellow officers, by treachery and cunning. Last year Aleman made the mistake of promoting him to general and naming him the head of the army. A month later Feliciano walked into the presidential palace with a squad of armed men and announced that he was taking over the government and that he had appointed Felipe Cardenas as the new president.

"My aunt, who works in the kitchen of the Presidencia, told me that one of the servants attending the president told her that when Aleman cried out, 'But you're like my son. How can you do this to me?' the general laughed in the old man's face."

García shook his head. "There are few who will mourn his passing, *señor*. Only those of his henchmen who stand to lose by his death. They're almost as dangerous as Feliciano. Until a new government takes over you and your woman are in danger. There will be patrols out looking for you. If anyone tries to stop you, don't hesitate to shoot."

"I won't," Tom said. "Believe me, I won't."

They stopped only briefly after that, and as soon as it was light, they found a place where they could rest and wait for dakness.

"I'll stand the first watch," Tom told the younger man. "You get some sleep."

"*Bueno, señor.* Wake me in four hours." With a nod to Rebecca, Enrique García turned away and found a place under one of the mango trees. Then, pulling his straw hat over his eyes, he went immediately to sleep.

But though she was tired, Rebecca didn't sleep. She sat next to Tom, and they talked in low tones so as not to wake the sleeping man.

"Are you feeling all right?" Tom asked. "This hasn't been too much for you?"

"I'm fine. Don't worry." She looked toward Enrique. "He spooked me when he was talking about that ten-thousand-dollar reward."

"Yeah, he spooked me, too. He's a nice young man. He reminds me of some of my students."

"And home?"

Tom nodded. "School will be starting soon. I always look forward to meeting the new students." He leaned back against the tree and let his thoughts travel to Brookfield Falls. Soon it would be autumn. The leaves would change color and the air would have a bite to it. He looked forward to his morning walk to the campus and he took pride in being a part of a college with a history like Brookfield's. Most of the gray stone buildings had been there from 1823 when the first part of the college had been built. It was steeped in tradition; it meant a great deal to him.

And he liked coming home at night to the welcoming smell of food coming from the kitchen and the crackle of logs in the fireplace. He looked forward to the way Melinda would rush down the stairs, eager to tell him everything that had happened to her that day.

"Melinda's birthday is in two weeks," he said.

"You'll make it." Rebecca reached for his hand.

"What do you buy an eleven-year-old girl for her birthday?"

"Clothes," she said with a laugh.

"I'm not good at that. A woman should buy a little girl's clothes."

Rebecca's laughter died. She had known that Tom had a daughter, but in a strange way she had really never thought of him as being a father. But he was, with all of the responsibilities being a parent entailed.

She thought of that day in the church when he told her he loved her, and though he hadn't said the words, she knew that love to Tom meant marriage, marriage and his daughter and his home. And God help her, that wasn't what she wanted. Not yet.

"I could ask Mrs. Plum to take her shopping," he said at last.

But Mrs. Plum had never had children. The one time he'd asked her to take Melinda shopping they'd returned with a navy-and-maroon dress that had long sleeves and came almost to Melinda's ankles. Melinda was in tears and she'd never worn the dress.

"Not clothes," he said. "Something else."

"Her own telephone?"

"Maybe. I guess she'd like that."

Then, because she was curious, Rebecca asked, "Do you have a picture of her?"

He shook his head. "They took everything away from me when I was captured. I had pictures of both Melinda and Beth. I asked for them back, but they wouldn't give them to me."

"Does Melinda look like you?"

"She has my eyes I think, but the rest of her features are more delicate, like Beth's."

Rebecca wanted to ask him about Beth, but she didn't. That was a part of Tom's life that had nothing to do with her, as her life with the agency had nothing to do with him. These days that they had shared had brought them close very quickly. She had told Tom that she loved him. And it was true; she did. But when this was over... No, she wouldn't think about that right now. There would be time later.

They sat in companionable silence for a little while, and when he said, "You'd better rest now," she curled up near him and went to sleep.

His thoughts drifted to Melinda and Beth. He remembered the first time he had seen Beth. She'd been running across the campus, long blond hair flying in the wind, clutching an armful of books. She'd been wearing a short green-and-black plaid skirt and a green sweater. He'd been watching her, thinking how pretty she was, when suddenly she stumbled and fell and the books went flying. He had hurried over to her and picked her up, then her books. And when, flustered, she had thanked him, he'd said, "My name is Tom Thornton."

A year later they were married. She'd been a wonderfully warm and caring woman, and she had given him the precious gift that was Melinda. He had loved her and he had grieved for her, and when she died, he had told himself that he would never marry again. But he knew now that he would if Rebecca would have him. He would always keep the memory of Beth close to his heart. But Beth was gone; it was time to love again.

He looked at Rebecca, asleep under the tree, one hand beneath her head, the other curled against her cheek. When this was over, he would take her back to Brookfield Falls. She would meet Melinda. And he would ask her to marry him.

In the early afternoon Enrique took over the watch from Tom. He ate one of the sandwiches Maria had packed and settled into a more comfortable position with his back against a tree.

It was almost dark when Tom felt a hand on his shoulder. Before he could speak Enrique whispered. "Soldiers. Be very quiet."

Tom sat up. Rebecca was already awake, the gun in her hand. Her face was white, tense. He heard a limb crack, and voices.

Enrique, crouching low, signaled for them to go ahead of him, then he followed, walking backward, brushing their tracks away as he came. Near an overhang of rocks he paused and looked around. There was an opening through the thickness of brush, not a cave, but a recess beneath the rocks.

"We'll hide here," Enrique said.

Beside him Tom felt Rebecca stiffen. He remembered how afraid she had been in the cave. This hole in the ground was worse. He knew how bad it would be for her, but they had no choice.

"It'll be all right," he told her. And to Enrique he said, "I'll go in first."

There was barely enough room for the three of them. When Enrique pulled the bushes close to the entrance, there was no light and very little air.

Tom put his arm around Rebecca's shoulders. "I'm with you," he murmured, and pulled her close.

It was difficult. Even before the incident in Caracas she had been afraid of dark, closed-in places, had been since that long-ago summer at the place in the Hamptons that her father owned. The summer that she was five one of her father's producer friends had come to spend a week with them. The friend had brought along his two children, a boy and a girl, both older than Rebecca. The boy had teased and called her

"Carrots" because of her hair. The girl, three years older than Rebecca, had teased, too, but her teasing, unlike her brothers, had been vicious and mean.

"My father said that your mother lives in California," she had said one day when Rebecca beat her at jacks. "He said she doesn't live with you or your father because she doesn't care anything about you and that she didn't even want you to get born."

Rebecca had flown at the other girl, fists doubled, crying, "That's a lie! That's a rotten dirty lie. Take it back!"

They'd grabbed her, brother on one side, sister on the other, and they'd shoved her into the closet beneath the back stairs and locked the door.

It was darker than any darkness she'd ever known. She'd heard the scurrying of mice and she'd pounded on the door until her hands were red and blistered. And the very worst thing of all, she'd been so terrified that she'd pee-peed on the floor.

Her father had finally heard her screams and rescued her. "Really, Rebecca," he said when he unlocked the door. "I didn't think you were such a baby."

This was like the closet. But this time she wasn't alone; she was with Tom. With him beside her she could face the darkness.

The voices of the men who were hunting for them came closer. Someone said, "There's no use looking. It's been over a week since the general's murder. The Americans have gone."

"Impossible," a voice answered. "How would they leave? The airport's been closed, the coast is patrolled and the port of entry is closed. They couldn't have escaped."

"The sentry they shot said he had hit the woman. Perhaps she's dead."

"They say she was very beautiful."

"Beautiful women were the general's weakness."

"This one cost him his life."

"*Sí, compañero.*" Someone laughed. "I hope she was worth dying for."

Tom cupped the back of Rebecca's head and held her close to his shoulder.

The voices receded. They waited. At last Enrique lifted the branches that covered the entrance and looked out. "They've gone. It's almost dark. It's safe now, but let me go first to make sure." He eased himself out of the hiding place.

"Are you all right?" Tom asked Rebecca.

"Yes, but I'll be glad to get out of here."

"Only a couple of minutes more."

Enrique pulled the bushes away from the entrance. "It's okay. Come on."

Tom went first, then reached to help Rebecca up and out. Her hair was disheveled and her face was dirty. Beneath the dirt he could see how pale she was. Without saying anything she reached for the canteen and took a drink, and he saw that her hands were shaking.

He thought of the kind of work she did, and knew from the time they had spent together that she wasn't at all the gung-ho woman he had first thought her to be. He had seen her vulnerabilities and her fears, as well as her strengths. He wondered, as he had before, what drove her to do the work she did. He knew how dangerous it was, what the odds of her coming out of an assignment alive were. And he knew, deep in his soul, that sooner or later those odds would catch up with her.

He loved her. He wanted to be with her and protect her. But he couldn't, not unless she gave up the work she did.

They went on, feeling their way in the darkness through the jungle growth until, a little after midnight, Rebecca stopped and put her hand on Tom's arm.

"What is it?" Tom asked. "Do you want to rest?"

She shook her head. "I can smell the sea."

"You're right," Enrique said with a nod. "We're close to the beach."

"If we can reach the shore while it's still dark, we can send a signal." She was excited now, sure that the worst was over. "We're not that far from the rendezvous point, Tom, so say a prayer that tonight's the night Ed Blakley comes back with the ship.

But it wasn't the night. When they reached the beach, she signaled with the flashlight again and again, hoping the beam of light could be seen by whoever might be waiting for them.

Enrique paced up and down the beach, and finally he said, "I don't like it. There are patrol boats guarding the coast. If one of them saw your light, they would know it was a signal. It's dangerous."

"Enrique's right," Tom said. "What we're doing *is* dangerous, Rebecca. What if there were soldiers camped on the beach and they saw your light?"

"But if we don't signal how will they know we're here?" she argued. "How will we ever get off the island?"

"You could get your own boat," Enrique suggested.

"Our own boat! That's ridiculous! That—"

"Maybe not," Tom said. "Enrique's right about the possibility of a patrol boat seeing the signal." He looked at her through the darkness. "And we've got to remember, Rebecca, that a lot of time has passed. Your people may have given up on us.'"

"No!" she said sharply. "I don't believe that. They're out there somewhere, waiting for a signal."

Tom rested a hand on her shoulder. Without replying he turned to Enrique. "What about a boat? Do you think there's a possibility of getting one?"

"Yes, I think so. Tomorrow I could go to Grenville. I've got a friend who works in a boat yard there. Maybe he'll know about something. Your best bet would be to head for the Mexican coast."

"I don't have any money," Tom said. "They took what I had when I was in prison."

"I have a couple of thousand dollars and a credit card," Rebecca put in, indicating the backpack Tom was carrying. "I can send the rest as soon as we're back in the States."

Enrique nodded. "I'll try to arrange something."

"Then it's settled. Rebecca and I will wait here until you return."

She frowned. Maybe Tom was right about the danger of sending a signal, but damn it, this was her operation. She was in charge. He had no right taking over for her.

He put his hand on her shoulder. "We'd better get some rest, honey."

She looked up at him, and suddenly it didn't seem to matter that he was taking charge, that he was making the decision. She felt his strength. She needed it. And him.

* * *

Enrique left at dawn after cautioning them to stay well back in the trees. But the day was quiet. There were no patrols, nothing to mar this perfect stretch of clean white sand, this momentary peace they had found. The water ran in unbelievable shades of deep dark blue, green and turquoise, depending on the movement of the clouds. At eventide the sky blazed with color, the sand looked pink, and the full white clouds were touched with fire.

It had been a beautiful day. "The most beautiful I've ever seen," Rebecca said.

All day she had longed to run down the beach into the water, but had known that she couldn't, that there was still the danger of soldiers patrolling the beach. When she said, "I'd love a swim," Tom shook his head.

"We can't take a chance," he said. "I'm afraid we'll just have to stay here and amuse ourselves any way we can." He drew her into his arms. "Put your mind to it, Rebecca. Try to think of something we can do."

She reached up under his T-shirt and began to caress his chest. "I'm thinking, I'm thinking."

"Of something more interesting than swimming?" He began to unbutton her shirt.

"Maybe." She rubbed her breasts against his chest. "What if Enrique comes back?"

"He won't until dark."

"You're sure?"

"Umm." He kissed her, and with his arms still around her brought her down onto the moss-covered earth beside him. "You taste so incredibly good."

She kissed his chest. "So do you."

"Undress me."

Her eyebrows went up. "I beg your pardon?"

"Undress me, Rebecca."

A smile tugged at the corners of her lips. "Work, work, work, that's all I do." She unfastened his belt and slowly pulled his zipper down. His manhood pushed hard against the black briefs, and she said, "My, oh, my. What have we here?" She ran her fingers down the length of the tumescence. "It's enough to frighten a lady to death, sir."

"Not this lady." He pulled her down to him, kissed her hard and deep and said, "Now finish what you've started."

She felt the flutter beat of her heart, and a flame that spread and grew from her belly down to that most secret part of her. With hands that shook in eagerness she eased the black briefs down over his legs. "Lift your hips," she whispered.

"Come over me," he said when he was naked.

But Rebecca waited, gazing down at him, marveling in his beauty. For he was beautiful—wide of shoulder and chest, narrow of waist and hips, long of leg. She touched the side of his face, then slowly, tenderly, began to run her hands down his body, lingering, caressing, stroking, loving him as she had never thought it possible to love.

He watched her face, saw the gentleness there, and the passion. And though his body cried out for the joining, he made himself wait until the waiting became unbearable and he said, "Please, Rebecca."

"Yes, my darling." She settled herself over him.

He felt the damp, sweet-smelling earth beneath his back, and he looked beyond her through the trees to the incredible blue of the sky. He heard the roll of the sea and its motion became his own. He touched her breasts. She shivered and closed her eyes. "No," he said. "Look at me when I touch you like this. Look at me, Rebecca."

Their cadence quickened. He thrust hard up against her, and when she whispered his name, he thought his heart would burst with loving her.

It started for her then, surged and surged again. Higher and still higher. And when his body exploded under hers, she cried out and collapsed against him, her heart beating like a captured bird's against his.

And in that moment of passion so intense that it was a little like dying Tom clasped her to him. "I'll never let you go," he whispered. "Not after this, Rebecca."

It was almost dark when they heard the low whistle coming from the water. They went down to the beach and through the mists of near darkness saw the sail-boat. Enrique waved and motioned for them to wait where they were.

"This is it." Tom put an arm around Rebecca's waist. They had shared so much on this island—cruelty and death, passion and love. He had found a happiness he had never expected to find; he had found Rebecca. He looked back to that place under the trees where they had made love today and felt a terrible sadness because, in a way he couldn't explain, he was afraid that once they left they would never again find what they had shared here.

"There's a part of me that doesn't want to leave," he said as he watched the boat come closer.

Rebecca rested her head on his shoulder. "I know," she whispered.

"When this is over, I want—"

She put her fingers over his lips. "It isn't over yet."

Enrique came in closer to shore and they got a better look at the fourteen-foot sailboat that looked as though it had seen better days. "Good Lord!" Tom shook his head. "We're going to try to make it to Mexico in that?"

"We can't, Tom," she said. "It's too small. We'd be swamped by the first big wave."

"I'll admit it doesn't look too good." He waded into the water, and when Enrique jumped out, he helped him pull the boat toward shore.

"This was the only thing I could find." Enrique shook his head. "What do you think?"

"I'd hate to trust it on the open sea," Tom said.

"Yes, that's what I thought, but..." Enrique looked uneasy. "I saw some lights farther on down the beach, Tom. They were headed this way."

Tom looked at Rebecca. "We don't have a choice. We've got to chance it. Get the backpack. We're shoving off."

"I put water and food in the boat," Enrique told him. "And a hat for the lady." He took his own hat off and handed it to Tom. "You'll need this."

Rebecca ran back to the beach. She didn't like the idea of the boat, but like Tom, she knew they didn't have any choice. Better to face the dangers of the sea than to risk the soldiers.

Tom took the backpack from her and tossed it into the boat. "Thanks for everything," he said to Enrique. He hesitated. "Have you ever thought about coming to the States?"

"Sure, lots of times. Maybe someday I'll even make it."

"How'd you like to go to college?"

"I'd like it fine if I were a millionaire."

Tom clamped his shoulder. "If we get out of this alive, I'll send for you. I'll see to it that you get into college. Okay?"

Enrique's face lit up. "Yes, I'd like that, Tom. Thanks!"

Rebecca gave him most of the money she had. "If it's more, tell your friend I'll be in touch with him through you or through Father Valverde."

Enrique took the money and grinned. "It won't be more, *señora*. The boat is hardly worth the nails that are holding it together."

"That's a comforting thought," she said.

Tom and Enrique shoved the boat off, and with a final wave of his hand, Tom climbed aboard.

Rebecca clutched the side of the boat. "Is there a motor?"

"A motor?" Tom shook his head. "We have a sail, milady," he said, trying to make light of it. "Why would we need a motor?"

"I guess ..." Rebecca swallowed hard. "I guess it's a nice night for a sail."

"That it is." He reached for her. "We're going to be all right. We're going to make it, Rebecca."

His face, shadowed by moonlight, was confident. The hand on the tiller was strong. She breathed deeply of the sea air and knew that whatever the peril that lay ahead she would rather be here with Tom than anywhere else in the world.

Chapter 14

They could see the campfires far back on the beach, so they ran without the running light and were silent for fear that their voices would carry over the water. At last when the fires faded, Tom said, "We're safe now."

"What about the patrols?"

"Without lights we'd see them before they saw us. I doubt they'd be more than a mile or two out. It'll be all right. Don't worry."

Don't worry? Rebecca shivered in the night air. The sea was dark and deep, and from somewhere in the past came the lines, "And I have miles to go before I sleep." She didn't know how far they were from the Yucatán Peninsula, but it had to be at least a hundred miles. They had no sailing charts, only the compass to guide them south. The boat was too small, unseaworthy. Even Enrique said it wasn't worth more than the nails that held it together.

Tom's hand was on the tiller. His face in the light of the half-moon was serious and strong. He looked as though he knew what he was doing.

"You've sailed before," she said.

"My folks had a cottage on Lake Winnebago in Wisconsin, and we had a boat there, not much bigger than this one. I learned to sail when I was fourteen, but it's been a long time since I handled a boat."

"However long it's been you know more than I do." She gave him a smile. "That makes you the captain, Captain."

Tom motioned her to the bench beside him, and when she moved closer, he put an arm around her shoulders and she leaned back against him. Only the sound of the waves against the hull and the slap of the sail in the wind broke the silence. There was a half-moon overhead and the sky was full of stars. Stars to navigate by.

"If we head due south, how long to you think it will take us to reach the Mexican coast?" she asked.

"A few days," he said, hedging. "But with any luck we'll be picked up by a fishing boat or a freighter long before that." He tightened his arm around her. "Maybe even by a luxury yacht that serves martinis before dinner."

"Hold that thought." Some of her earlier fear had faded. They weren't home free yet, but they'd gotten away from San Sebastian and they had enough food and water to last for several days. If their luck held out . . . She yawned.

"There's a tarpaulin in the bottom of the boat," Tom said. "Why don't you spread that out and try to get some sleep?"

"Maybe I will." She moved away from him and stretched. "Wake me in a couple of hours so I can take over."

"I will."

She leaned over to kiss him, and he put his arm around her waist. "We're going to be all right, Rebecca."

She cradled his head against her breast. "I know, Tom. I know."

The bottom of the boat was ribbed and hard and it smelled of stale fish. But finally Rebecca found a reasonably comfortable position and closed her eyes. When she opened them again, the moon had moved. It was time to relieve Tom.

She got up, and though he protested, she insisted he show her what to do and what stars to navigate by. "Wake me in two hours," he said.

But she didn't. She let him sleep, and it was dawn before he awoke. Over a breakfast of fruit and canned tuna Rebecca said, "I'll never eat another tuna fish sandwich for as long as I live."

"Or canned beans." Tom grinned and handed her one of the bottles of water.

"How much do we have?" she asked.

"Enough."

"How much?"

"Three bottles."

"We'd better be careful with it. In case."

He took a sip.

"It's a nice day," she said.

He looked up at the sun. It was going to be nice all right, he thought, nice and hot.

He was right. By noon the temperature had risen to over a hundred degrees and the sun burned down with blazing fierceness. The straw hats Enrique had given them helped, but Rebecca's shirt stuck to her back and her face was beaded with sweat. The heat was inescapable, smothering, smoldering. It weakened them. It made them thirst for more water than they knew they should drink.

Tom rigged the tarp overhead. "That'll help."

Rebecca tilted the straw hat lower over her face. She felt as though she could drink a gallon of water but knew she couldn't, that they had to ration every drop.

What breeze there had been earlier lessened and died. The sail sagged, and the boat slowed and drifted almost without motion. There was no land, nothing for as far as the eye could see except this great expanse of sea.

They sat in the bottom of the boat, near the tiller under the tarp. "It'll be better when the sun goes down," Tom said. "Maybe the wind will pick up then."

"What do other sailors do when the sea's calm like this?" Rebecca asked.

"Just what we're doing. They wait."

Her mouth was dry. She closed her eyes.

"What are you thinking about?" he asked.

"Iced tea with a lots of ice cubes."

"Think up a glass for me." He reached for the water. "Take a few sips. You need it."

The sun got hotter, the air more still as the afternoon wore on. The sunset was beautiful, and at the last moment there came that phenomenon known as the green flash, one stunning flash of green across the fading blue and dazzling red of the sky just before the sun sank from view.

"It'll be cooler now," Tom said. "We should get a breeze, too."

But the breeze didn't come. They stayed becalmed that whole night, the tiller useless as they drifted on the tide. They lay side by side on the tarp they'd used as an awning, both of them worried, both of them talking of other things.

Long after Rebecca had fallen asleep Tom lay looking up at the stars. He had heard of boats that had been becalmed for days, even weeks. If that happened, they couldn't survive. They didn't have enough food or water. Even if the wind came up, they had lost a day. Their only hope now was that a passing ship would pick them up.

He reached out and took Rebecca's hand. Her fingers curled around his and at last he slept.

The wind started just before morning. The sail billowed and the small boat skimmed across the waves. Rebecca, braced against the roll, red hair blowing back from her face, laughed and said, "This is wonderful. It'll blow us all the way to Yucatán."

Heavy clouds scudded across the leaden sky and there was the smell of a storm in the air. Again and again Tom scanned the horizon, hoping, praying for a ship. But there was only the endless expanse of the deep, threatening sea.

By afternoon the waves were higher and water sloshed over the side of the boat. With the empty can of beans they'd had for lunch, Rebecca bailed, her earlier exuberance forgotten in this new and frightening development. The heavy roll of the waves made her dizzy and her stomach felt queasy. She'd always thought that seasickness was a problem of mind over matter. But this wasn't in her mind; it was in her stomach. She'd heard that if you focused on something steady it helped. But there wasn't anything steady. Everything kept rolling, roiling, bobbing up and down, up and down... She leaned over the side of the boat and was retchingly sick.

Tom wanted to help her, but he couldn't take his hand off the tiller. All he could do was say, "Take a couple of deep breaths, honey. That'll help."

She managed to nod, took a deep breath and kept bailing.

The wind grew stronger, the waves so high that each time the small boat climbed one Tom held his breath. There were no life jackets aboard. If they were swamped, there would be little chance of survival. They were both soaking wet. Again and again Rebecca had to put her head over the side. Her face was pale, but she kept bailing.

Night came. The wind lessened, but the sea was still rough. She lay in the bottom of the boat in half an inch of water, too exhausted to move. Tom tied the tiller in place with a strip torn from his shirt and went to her. He held the bottle of water to her lips. "You have to drink," he said.

"Can't hold it down."

"Yes, you can. Come on, Rebecca. Take a couple of sips."

She made herself do what he asked, then lay back, eyes closed.

"You'll feel better if you go to sleep," he said.

"I'm never going to feel better. If we ever get off this damn boat, I'll never set foot on another one for as long as I live."

He wiped her damp hair back from her forehead. "There aren't any oceans in Illinois."

He went back to the tiller and stayed there all that long night, his eyes forever searching for a ship's light, or land. Because he knew that without help they couldn't last another day.

He awoke with a start, his hand still on the tiller, his head resting against the side of the boat. The sea was calmer, but the clouds were dark and heavy with threatened rain. He looked at Rebecca, asleep on the tarp at the bottom of the boat. I wanted to spend the rest of my life with you, he thought. I wanted to live with you and grow old with you. I wanted to have children with you. He ran a hand across his whiskered jaw. I wanted a lifetime with you Rebecca, he thought. I wanted... He raised his head to look out at the roiling gray water. Suddenly his eyes narrowed and a cry escaped his lips, for there, riding high on the crest of the waves, he saw a boat.

"Rebecca!" he cried. "Rebecca!"

She sat up, groggy, clutching the side of the boat for support.

"There's a boat! Get the tarp!"

"A boat?" She struggled to her knees, yanked the tarpaulin from under her, then staggered to her feet. "Where?" she asked. "Where?"

Tom pointed to his right. "There, you see? Wait till the wave crests. There it is."

She began to scream, "Help! We're over here. Help! Help!"

He grabbed the tarp from her hands and waved it, shouting as she did, "Help. Over here! Help!"

The boat moved farther away, but he kept waving as his voice screamed out over the waves. Suddenly the boat seemed to stop and hover on the waves. Then it turned and started toward them.

"They're coming!" Tears were running down Rebecca's face. "Tom, they're coming!"

Over the water came a shout. "*¡Ah, del barco!* Ahoy the boat!"

They saw the Mexican flag. Tom dropped the tarpaulin and put his arms around Rebecca. "It's all right now. It's over, Rebecca. We're safe."

Two days later the fishing boat that had picked them up reached the port of Progreso on the Yucatán Peninsula. From there it was less than an hour to the city of Mérida, and a hospital with clean sheets on the bed, sweet-faced nurses and a doctor who said, "You are dehydrated, *Señorita*. All you need is to rest and take fluids. Tomorrow you will be better."

"Tom? Professor Thornton?"

"He is fine, but he is asleep. As soon as he awakens I will let him see you."

She slept, and when she awoke, Tom was sitting beside her and Alexander Hayden was standing at the foot of her bed.

"Alex?" She raised herself to a sitting position. "What are you doing here?"

"What do you think I'm doing here? The professor called me last night and I flew in this morning."

"He hates to be called 'Professor'." She smiled up at Tom.

"Only by you," he said.

Hayden's bushy eyebrows shot up.

"How do you feel?" Tom asked.

"Better. Hungry."

"That's a good sign. The doctor said what you needed now was a month's rest and lots of TLC." He squeezed her hand. "Tender loving care is my specialty."

Hayden cleared his throat. "We need to have a briefing."

"As soon as Rebecca's feeling better." Tom stood and faced the other man. "She's had almost five weeks of hell, thanks to you. She needs time to recuperate."

"She can recuperate in Washington."

Tom shook his head. "No. She's coming back to Brookfield Falls with me."

"Now just one damn minute, Thornton. You can't come in here and take over. Rebecca works for me."

"Tom," Rebecca tried to say. "Tom, I can't . . ."

He ignored her protest. "The doctor said he'd release her tomorrow," he told Hayden. "We'll check into a hotel as soon as she's out of here. She'll see you in the afternoon. I've given you the film and the tape of the notes I took. That should hold you until you see her tomorrow."

Hayden's cheeks puffed out and his face got red. "See here," he roared. "I won't have you or anybody else telling me what she will or won't do. She saved your life—"

"I know that."

"And by God I *am* going to talk to her. Right now!"

"Not by God or by anything else," Tom said, standing his ground.

"Damn it, Thornton, I represent the government of the United States—"

"We're in Mexico now."

Hayden's eyes blazed. He glared down at Rebecca. "Tell him," he ordered. "Tell this macho professor of yours that I have to talk to you now. There's been a shake-up in San Sebastian and I need details, facts."

She looked at Tom. "This really is important."

"So is your health." Tom stepped to the door and opened it. "Tomorrow," he told the other man.

Hayden started to say something. Then his mouth snapped shut. He glared at Tom, then at Rebecca. "You never let anybody tell you what to do before," he told her.

"Only you, Alex." She held out her hand to him. "I really am very tired."

A muscle jumped in his cheek. "All right," he snapped. "Tomorrow then."

"The Hotel Casa del Balam," Tom said. "Four o'clock?"

If Hayden had had a cigar in his mouth, he would have bitten it in half. "Four," he growled, and left.

Tom sat back down on the side of the bed and took Rebecca's hand. "I don't think your boss likes me."

"He's not used to having anybody disagree with him." She chuckled. "All this time he's thought of you as a mild-mannered professor, and suddenly you've turned into a lion. That shook him." She squeezed his hand. "I really do have to go back to Washington, Tom."

"No, you don't. You're coming home with me even if I have to hog-tie you."

"But—"

He kissed her, silencing the words he didn't want to hear. "I phoned home last night," he said when he let her go. "Melinda's anxious to meet you. She said to tell you she'd bake chocolate chip cookies. Mrs. Plum is going to prepare the guest room and—"

"Tom, I can't."

"Yes, you can." He hesitated. "I'm not asking you to make any till-death-do-us-part kind of a commitment, Rebecca. I'm not going to pressure you into anything you're not ready for. I just want to take care of you. You need a vacation, and Brookfield Falls is beautiful this time of year. Melinda will be back in school and I'll be at the college. Mrs. Plum will see to your needs. You won't even have to cook."

"Tom, I...I don't know. I don't think I should. You and I have been through so much together these past weeks—"

"Which is exactly the point. You saved my life, Rebecca. Now let me do something for you. We'll see Hayden tomorrow, and the following day we'll fly to Chicago. Brookfield Falls is only an hour's drive from there."

"Listen to me for a minute." She sat up in bed, her face serious, her eyes stormy. "You can't just take over like this. You can't—"

"Yes, I can." He put his arms around her back and drew her to him. He kissed her, a hard, serious kiss. "Yes, I can," he said again.

"*You* killed Feliciano?"

"I didn't mean to," Rebecca said. "It was an accident. We were struggling for the gun."

She told him then about her capture, about the trek through the jungle to the camp where Feliciano had set up his search headquarters. "He would have killed me," she told Hayden. "After he had no more use for me, after he turned me over to his men."

Hayden's face tightened. "I'm sorry, Rebecca. I didn't know, didn't realize how bad it had been for you."

"He would have done all the things he'd said he would do if it hadn't been for Tom. When I was captured, I hoped that Tom would make it to the rendezvous point because I wanted him to play it safe. But he didn't play it safe, Alex. He came after me. He followed the men who had me, and when he found the headquarters camp, he started a diversionary fire and came charging into Feliciano's camp like Grant taking Richmond. Feliciano tried to kill him. Instead I killed Feliciano."

She took a sip from a tall glass of iced tea. "We ran out of camp while most of the soldiers were fighting the fire, but one of the guards saw us and started shooting. I took a bullet in the leg."

"Rebecca, I didn't know. I—"

"Tom carried me, Alex. He carried me to a village and he dug the bullet out of my leg."

Hayden swung his gaze to Tom.

"She almost died." Tom reached for Rebecca's hand. "The village priest gave her the last rites."

Hayden got up. He strode to the window, hands behind his back, and looked down at the pool. Without turning he said, "Ed Blakley wanted to go to San Sebastian in your place. I should have let him. I shouldn't have sent you."

"But I was the right person for the job, Alex. You knew it. That's why you sent me. Ed's a good man, your *best* man, but he couldn't have gotten Tom out." She went over to the window and put a hand on Hayden's arm. "I was the only one who could have, Alex. You had to send me."

He put his arms around her and pulled her close. "You're like the daughter I never had," he said gruffly. "I hated sending you to San Sebastian, especially so soon after Caracas. I felt like a real son of a bitch, but I had to do it."

She smiled up at him. "And you'll do it again if you have to, Alex, because I'm good."

"Damn right you're good." He looked over her shoulder at Tom. "I didn't know about her being shot. Sorry."

Tom nodded. He still wasn't sure that he liked Hayden, but he could see the obvious affection that existed between Rebecca and her boss. But he was damned if he'd give in to Hayden about Rebecca's going back to Washington. He'd put up a fight about that.

"The Cardenas government has crumbled," Hayden told them. "Aleman has returned and things seem to be stabilizing. We've scheduled a meeting next week between our minister of defense and theirs concerning the missiles, but President Aleman has already assured us that the missile base will be dismantled. He's also said that we can send our own men in to help with the dismantling."

He looked at Tom. "We wouldn't have known anything about the missiles if it hadn't been for you, Professor Thornton. You knew what they were and you used your head in getting the film out." He offered Tom his hand. "Thank you on behalf of our government. And I want to thank you personally for taking care of Rebecca. She means a great deal to me, to all of us."

"To all of us," Tom said.

"And I'm sorry as hell, but I really must take her back to Washington. There will be others who'll want to question her about San Sebastian. However, I'll personally assure you that when it's all over she'll get a well-deserved rest."

"The way she did after Caracas?" Tom shook his head. "No, Hayden. Rebecca's coming to Brookfield Falls with me."

Hayden's jaw tightened. "Suppose we leave that up to Rebecca." He turned to her. "Well?" he asked.

She looked at him, then at Tom, lower lip caught between her teeth. Alex was right. She should go back to Washington. There were loose ends to pick up, other briefings, probably with the defense minister, a senatorial committee.

But she needed a rest, time to heal, both physically and emotionally from all that had happened in the past few weeks. And more important, she wasn't ready to say goodbye to Tom. She'd never be able to live the kind of life he would expect her to live if they married, and though he hadn't asked her to marry him, she knew from everything he had said that he'd thought about it. Tom Thornton wasn't a frivolous man. He had told her that he loved her, and for him love and marriage were synonymous. Perhaps this time together in his environment would be a way of showing both of them why she would never be able to settle down in Small Town, U.S.A.

The two men were watching her. Waiting.

"I want to go with Tom," she said. And because she wanted Tom to know that it would be a temporary thing, she said to Alex, "For a month, Alex. That's all I'm asking for. If there are any more questions, anything you or anybody else needs to know, you can call me at Tom's."

One month, Tom thought. It wasn't what he had hoped for, but it would have to do. It would give him time. And once she was in Brookfield Falls, once she had seen the town, his home, and when she met Melinda, perhaps it would be different.

He'd give her all the time she needed. He wouldn't press, wouldn't demand. But he would never give up hope that one day she would be his.

They send down for dinner and ate in the room. When Hayden left, he shook hands with Tom. "There are people in Washington who might need more information," he said.

"I'll be glad to do anything I can." Tom said. "Call me anytime."

Hayden nodded. To Rebecca he said, "Walk me to the door." And he put her arm through his. When they were out of earshot, he kissed her cheek and said, "The professor's quite a man."

"Yes, he is."

"I don't think he has a wimpish bone in his body." She laughed, and he laughed with her. Then his face sobered and he said, "He's in love with you, Becky."

"I know."

"You love him?"

"Yes, Alex."

"But you're not going to let him talk you into staying in Hooterville, are you?"

She took a deep breath. "No, I won't let him talk me into staying."

"Good girl."

But even as he said the words, there was something in Hayden's eyes that Rebecca had never seen before, a look of sadness, a shading of doubt. For a moment she felt that same sadness and doubt. And shrugged it off.

"A month," she said. "I'll be back to work in a month."

Chapter 15

Even without Tom's telling her Rebecca would have recognized the house from the way he had talked about it in San Sebastian. Like the other houses on the block, it was set well back from the tree-lined street, and it was white with gray shingles and shutters as many of them were. But unlike the other houses, the door was a bright sky-blue. And that made her smile.

Tom got out of the car he had rented at the airport in Chicago and came around to her side to help her out. "Home sweet home," he said as he took her hand.

Rebecca hesitated, suddenly shy, overcome with a what-am-I-doing-here feeling. Brookfield Falls was so different from what she was accustomed to. Everything about it—the maple trees that lined the street, the flowers in the front yards, marigolds and mums, phlox and peonies, the white picket fences—was all so . . . so Currier and Ives. She felt out of place, disoriented. She missed the rush of traffic, the discordant blare of horns, the screech of tires, the hubbub of big-city people rushing around.

The countryside, once they had left Chicago, had the look of early fall. The trees had already started changing, and there was a crisp, cool feeling to the air.

"We could have stayed on the highway," Tom had said, "but on a day like this I'd rather take the back roads."

Past farms with red barns and signs that read Fresh Chickens and Eggs, past rows of corn and fields of purple thistles, past rail fences and white-faced cows on the crest of green hills.

"It's good to be home," he said.

Home for him; it could never be home for her.

Now she looked at the white house with the blue door. I'll only stay for a few days, she told herself. I'll make an excuse. I'll . . . The door opened and a little girl came flying down the pebble walk, shouting, "Dad! You're here! You're here!"

She launched herself at him, and he picked her up and swung her off her feet. "Mellie," he said, hugging her tightly. "Let me look at you." He kissed both her cheeks, then held her away. "You're grown. You look—" he tweaked one of her braids "—almost grown-up," he finished.

"I'll be eleven on Sunday." Her thin arms tightened around his neck. "I was so afraid you wouldn't make it home for my birthday, Daddy."

"Neither wind nor rain nor sleet nor snow would ever keep me from my girl's birthday." He set her down. Then, holding her hand, he said, "Mellie, this is Miss Bliss. I told you about her on the phone."

Candid blue eyes looked up at her. A small hand was offered. A formal "How do you do?" was said.

"How do you do?" Rebecca took a deep breath. "I like your blue door."

"You do?" Melinda looked triumphantly up at her father, then back at Rebecca. "He didn't want to paint it blue. He wanted our house to be just like everybody else's house on the block, but I wanted it to be different." She reached for Rebecca's travel case. "We'd better go in. Mrs. Plum has been in a nervous twitchet all day because she's so curious to know what you look like she can barely stand it." She shot Rebecca a grin. "You're going to knock the starch right out of her 'cause you're just about the prettiest looking woman I've ever seen. Wait'll she—"

"Melinda . . ."

She sighed a long and painful sigh. "Sometimes Dad says I talk too much," she told Rebecca. "But the only time I do it is when I'm excited, like now. The rest of the time I'm pretty quiet." She took Rebecca's hand and started up the walk. "Do you have any kids?" she asked.

Rebecca shook her head. "I'm not married."

"Never been?"

Tom put his hand on her shoulder. "It isn't polite to ask questions. Run and tell Mrs. Plum we're here."

"She already knows. She looked through the curtain as soon as you got out of the car."

He turned to Rebecca and shook his head. "I thought the twos were the terrible years," he said with a grin.

Once in the house he called out, "Mrs. Plum. We're here."

She came out of the kitchen, wiping her hands on her apron, a small round woman in her seventies, short white hair in pixie points around her face, funny little cowlicks at the back of her head. Her cheeks were pink from the heat of the kitchen and her eyes were cornflower-blue.

"Well, here you are at last," she said in what to Rebecca was a perfectly charming English accent. "Melinda and I have been worried about you, sir. You're a bit thinner, aren't you? But not to worry. We'll fix that up in no time at all." She took one of the suitcases from him. "I've tried to keep things going the way you would have liked me to, but it wasn't the same without you. Both Melinda and I missed you a great deal."

Tom put an arm around Mrs. Plum's shoulders. "One of the things that helped keep me going was knowing that you were here with Melinda. I'm very grateful, Mrs. Plum. More grateful than I can tell you." He turned to Rebecca. "I'd like you to meet Rebecca Bliss. She's the one who rescued me and brought me safely home. She's been ill and needs looking after."

"Bliss. Now isn't that a dearie name?" Mrs. Plum held out her hand and shook Rebecca's. "I've fixed up the guest room real nice and cheery, Miss Bliss. It's the room overlooking the backyard. Lots of trees there and still some wee flowers in bloom. It's quiet as ever a room could be, so you can sleep till noon every day if you've a mind to."

"I just might do that." Some of Rebecca's tension eased. She smiled at Mrs. Plum, then looked around the big living room. There were crisscross curtains at the windows, dark green deep-piled carpeting, a fireplace where two tweedish and comfortable-looking sofas sat facing each other. There were easy chairs and recliners, lamps and end tables with framed photographs, walls lined with floor-to-ceiling bookcases, a piano. The room looked lived in and homey.

Tom's home.

"I'm the one who plays the piano," Melinda said. "Dad said that my mother did, too, but I don't remember. Do you know how to play, Rebecca?"

Rebecca shook her head. "But I'm pretty good at putting on a compact disc," she said.

Melinda's giggle filled the room. "Dad got me a CD player last Christmas and I love it. He doesn't like the music I play, though. He doesn't even like the New Kids on the Block. Want me to show you your room?"

"Yes, that would be nice." And to Tom she said, "I'd like to clean up and have a bit of a rest if that's all right."

"Take you time. Dinner's at . . . ?" He looked at Mrs. Plum.

"At seven," she said. "But I can hold it if you're resting, Miss Bliss."

"Seven will be fine," Rebecca answered.

Tom picked up her suitcase, and Melinda led the way up the stairs. "This is your room," she said when she opened a door at the end of the hall.

It was a large room, sunny and bright. A patchwork quilt covered the four-poster bed. There was a wicker rocker in one corner, a dressing table and a dresser with a bouquet of marigolds on it.

"I picked the flowers," Melinda said.

"Did you?" Rebecca smiled. "Thank you, Melinda. Marigolds are my favorites."

"Mine, too."

Tom rested his hand on his daughter's shoulder. "It was nice of you to think of it. We'd better let Rebecca rest now. It was a long trip from Mexico, and she's tired." He hesitated, then kissed Rebecca's cheek. "Sleep as long as you want to. Dinner can wait."

When she was alone, she looked around the room, then sank down onto the bed and leaned her head against the bedpost. She had known before that she and Tom came from different backgrounds, but until now she hadn't realized how true that was. And it wasn't just Tom; he came equipped with a ready-made family, a hundred-year-old house, a housekeeper and a whole way of life that was vastly different than her own. This was where he belonged, but she didn't.

She decided then that tomorrow she would phone Alex and tell him she'd changed her mind, that she was coming back to Washington. She'd call her father, too. Alex had told her when he came to Mexico that he had spoken with her father as soon she he'd gotten word that she was safe. "He would have come to Mexico with me," Alex had told her. "But he's having problems with the new sitcom."

"It's all right," she'd said. "I understand."

And she did. Her father's career came first. It always had; it always would. He didn't know what kind of work she did, only that she worked for Alex and that she traveled a lot. If he surmised what it was, he never questioned, nor did she volunteer any information. It was better that way for both of them.

She slipped off her shoes and lay back on the bed. And as she looked around the room, she wondered what it would have been like, growing up in a house like this, in a town like this. What would it have been like to go to high school dances with a boy like Tom?

To kiss in the moonlight, to marry and have children, to live and grow old in this house.

With a man like Tom.

With thoughts of him, and the way it might have been, she closed her eyes and slept.

Mrs. Plum fixed an old-fashioned pot roast with potatoes, carrots and onions for dinner. There was rich brown gravy, a plate of celery and olives, a green salad with a real Roquefort cheese dressing. And candles on the table.

Melinda had changed from the blue jeans and shirt she'd worn earlier to a light green dress with white collar and cuffs. "I don't usually dress up for dinner," she said in an aside to Rebecca. "But this is a special occasion."

"Yes, it is." Tom took her hand, then Rebecca's. "Would you say the blessing, Mellie?"

Looking suddenly shy, Melinda bobbed her head and raced through, "Bless us, O Lord, and these Thy gifts, which we are about to receive from Thy bounty. Amen." Then she took a deep breath and said, "And thank you for bringing Dad and Miss Bliss back safely."

Tom squeezed her hand. "Thank you, sprite." He smiled across the table at Rebecca. "Family custom. Hope you don't mind."

"No, it's...it's very nice." And very different. Her father had never said grace at meals. Actually he'd rarely been home for meals. Growing up, she'd either had her dinner alone at the big dining room table that was seldom used except for the dinner parties her father sometimes had, or in front of the TV. This family gathering, this closeness, was something she wasn't used to.

Melinda carried most of the conversation at dinner, and Rebecca was content to watch the warmth and interaction between father and daughter. She told him everything that had happened since he'd been away—about a neighbor who'd been rushed to the hospital with appendicitis, about her best friend Susanna who, when she found out she had to wear braces on her teeth, had demanded a bra by way of compensation. And then, with a hopeful look, she told him about Sammy Parson's dog having puppies. "Collie puppies," she said wistfully.

Tom listened. That was what impressed Rebecca the most. He really listened to everything his daughter said.

For dessert there was ice cream and the chocolate chip cookies Melinda had made. "As a sorta welcome home," the little girl said.

When dinner was finished, the three of them went into the living room. Melinda asked questions about San Sebastian. "Were you really in prison there?" she asked Tom. "Was it terrible?"

"It was pretty bad," he told her truthfully.

"And Miss Bliss rescued you!" She looked at Rebecca. "That's the most exciting, the most *romantic* thing I've ever heard. It's like you're a lady detective, or a spy." Her eyes widened. "Are you a spy, Miss Bliss?"

Rebecca shook her head. "No," she said. I'm not a spy. I work for a government agency that's kind of like the FBI."

"Wow! And you rescued Dad with guns blazing . . ." She stopped. "Did you ever kill anybody?"

Before Rebecca could answer Tom said, "It's late, Melinda. Time for bed."

"But, Dad—"

"No argument, sprite."

She sighed a long, painful sigh, then got up and went to Tom. "Night, Dad," she said, and kissed his cheek. She hesitated for a moment, then quickly bent and kissed Rebecca.

The kiss was shy, tentatively given, and very sweet. It clutched at Rebecca's heart and made her long for some indescribable thing she had never known. She wanted to put her arms around this child, to rub her back and smooth her hair. She wanted... "Good... good night," she managed to say. "Sleep well."

"Good night, Miss Bliss."

"How about calling me Rebecca?"

"I'd like that. Or Becky. That's really cute. How about Becky?"

"Becky's fine."

"Then that's what I'll call you. Tomorrow's Saturday, so I don't have school, but Dad has to go to the college. Maybe I could show you around." She headed for the stairs. "Right after breakfast. Okay?"

"Okay," Rebecca said.

"Becky?" Tom raised an eyebrow. "I thought you didn't like anybody calling you Becky."

"Well... Melinda's special." She smiled at him. "She really is special, Tom. You've done a wonderful job with her."

"It was easy. She's a great kid."

But Rebecca knew it hadn't been easy raising a child alone, especially a little girl. Tom was a loving man. She had seen it before when he had cared for her, and she saw it now with his daughter. The affection and love between father and daughter was very real, very strong. He was an exceptional man, and as she looked at him sitting in a comfortable armchair with the light of the lamp reflecting on his face, she thought, Be careful, Rebecca. Be very careful or you're going to find yourself buying into this family bit. It isn't your style of living. It isn't for you.

She looked at Tom, and when she saw him looking at her, she lowered her eyes.

Her face had changed when Mellie kissed her, he thought. She'd gone suddenly still, then tentatively she had put an arm around Mellie's shoulders. Now there was an expression in her eyes he had never seen before, and it seemed to Tom he could almost see the conflicting emotions that troubled her.

He was glad she had come home with him. It was strange and somehow very right to see her sitting here on the sofa with her shoes off and her feet curled under her. This is where you belong, he wanted to tell her. Here with Melinda and with me. Don't you see that? Don't you see how it would be if you were with us?

He thought, too, of how it would be to turn out the lights and go up the stairs with her to a room that was theirs. To lie with her there, to love with her there. To awake in the morning with her beside him.

He wanted to tell her all those things, but because he knew it was too soon he said, "It's late, Rebecca, and you're tired. Why don't you go up now?" He got to his feet, took her hand and brought her up beside him. "I'm so glad you're here," he told her. And though he wanted to, he didn't say, This is where you belong. Instead, he said, "I have to go to the college in the morning. You sleep as late as you want to. I'll tell Mellie not to wake you." He drew her to him and kissed her. "Good night, my dear."

"Good night, Tom."

She hesitated. He thought she wanted to say something else, but she didn't. She only looked at him for a moment, then turned and went up the stairs.

But it was a long time before Tom went up to bed. He leaned back in the chair and closed his eyes. He thought of how it would be if Rebecca were his wife. And knew that soon he would ask her.

Rebecca awakened with the chirping of birds in the maple tree outside the bedroom window. Sun filtered in through the open drapes, warming the room. She snuggled down under the patchwork quilt, for though it was only the middle of September there was a chill to the morning air. After the heat of San Sebastian, it felt good to be cool, and she had slept through the night without waking.

The smell of bacon frying drifted up from below and, realizing that she was hungry, she threw back the covers and got out of bed. The minute her feet hit the floor there was a knock and a small voice said, "Becky? Are you awake, Becky?"

Rebecca gathered her robe around her shoulders and opened the door. Melinda stood there. She was dressed in blue jeans and a red-and-white-checked shirt. Her hair hung in two neat braids down her back and her face looked rosy and clean.

"Yes, I'm awake," Rebecca said. "Good morning."

"Good morning. I told Mrs. Plum to start breakfast. Is that okay? And after we eat we could go out for a while. Dad left the car and I can show you where I go to school and stuff like that. If you'd like to, I mean."

"I'd like to. Will you tell Mrs. Plum that I'll be down in about fifteen minutes?" Rebecca smiled. "Can you wait that long for breakfast?"

Melinda smiled back, and suddenly the room was even brighter and warmer than it had been before. Rebecca rested her hand for a moment on Melinda's head and asked, "Do you think it would be all right if I wore jeans, too?"

"Sure. All the mothers do."

Again there was that strange clutching at Rebecca's heart. "Well," she said. "Well, okay. You run along. I'll be downstairs in a little while."

When she closed the door, she leaned against it. Be careful, she told herself. Be very careful.

"Tomorrow's your birthday," Rebecca said when they got into the car. "I'd like to buy you a present. I thought maybe a party dress, but it depends on you. What would you like?"

"A party dress? Really?" Melinda's eyes widened. "Really."

"I'd love it! A blue dress with puffed sleeves. I'll wear it for my birthday tomorrow."

"We'll do our best to find you one," Rebecca promised as she backed the car out of the driveway. "You're the guide. You tell me where to go."

"That way," Melinda said, pointing, then fastening her seat belt. "That's the way to the mall."

"The mall it is."

There were two children's shops as well as a department store in the mall. They tried the department store first, and though there were several dresses Melinda thought were "kinda pretty," they couldn't find a blue one with puffed sleeves. Nor did they find it in the first children's shop they went to. But in the second shop they found exactly the dress Melinda had described.

"Ohh," Melinda said. "Isn't that the prettiest dress you've ever seen in your whole life?"

"It certainly is." Rebecca smiled, motioned to a saleslady and asked, "Do you have this dress in her size?"

"I'm not sure. Let me look."

Melinda clasped Rebecca's hand. "I'll die if they don't have it," she whispered.

But they did have it. Melinda asked Rebecca to come into the dressing room with her when she tried it on. "It's perfect," she said when she pulled it over her head. But when she looked at herself in the mirror her face fell.

"It's too long," she wailed. "Look, Becky, it's yards too long."

"We can have it fixed, honey. Don't worry. It's going to be fine."

The saleswoman stuck her head in the doorway. "Is everything all right? Oh, my, isn't that just lovely on you."

"It's a little long," Rebecca said. "We'd like it shortened."

"I think it's just fine the way it is, but, of course, if your daughter wants it shorter, I can get the alteration person. I'm sure she can have it for you by the middle of next week."

"I'm afraid we have to have it before that," Rebecca said in her firmest, no-nonsense voice. "Melinda's birthday is tomorrow. Surely the hem can be fixed in an hour or two. I'll be happy to pay any extra charge."

"Well…" The woman nodded. "Very well. Let me call alterations."

"You did it!" Melinda said when the woman left. She threw her arms around Rebecca. "Thank you, Becky. Thank you a million times."

"You're welcome, sweetheart."

"She thought you were my mom."

"Yes, I…I guess she did." Rebecca cleared her throat. "We'll probably have to wait an hour or two for them to fix the dress. What would you like to do while we're waiting?"

"Get my hair fixed so that it looks like yours." And before Rebecca could object Melinda rushed on. "I'm going to be eleven tomorrow and I'm sick of braids. I want my hair to be all soft and fluffy the way yours is."

"Your father might not like—"

"He won't care. Really he won't. It's Mrs. Plum who fixes my hair this way. I love her, Becky. She's really nice and everything, but she's not…like modern. You know?"

"I know, Melinda. But, honestly, I think we should ask your father before we do anything to your hair."

"It'll be all right with him. Honest it will. And I won't have it cut too short. Okay, Becky? Okay?"

Melinda was looking at her so hopefully that she was hard to resist. "We'll see what a beautician says," Rebecca said. "But no promises. Okay?"

Melinda breathed a sigh of relief. "Okay."

They found a shop with a pretty young woman who had a free hour. She undid Melinda's braids and brushed out her hair. "Your hair has a natural curl," she told Melinda. "If we took off five or six inches, it would be soft around your face and it would still be long enough for a pontytail in case you wanted to pull it back. I've got time to do it, but it's up to you and your mother."

"I'm not . . ." Rebecca started to say, then stopped. "It's up to you, Melinda."

Melinda gripped the arms of the chair. "Cut it," she said.

Blond hair drifted to the floor. Melinda squeezed her eyes shut. She opened them when it was done and time to shampoo her hair. She looked scared, but she didn't say anything until her hair was dry and brushed.

The beautician rested her hands on Melinda's shoulders. "What do you think?"

"It's beautiful!" The little girl turned a radiant face to Rebecca. "What do you think, Becky?"

"I think *you're* beautiful," Rebecca said. "And I think your dad's going to love it."

When they left the beauty salon, Melinda said, "I hope Dad's not home when we get there. I'd like to be wearing my new dress when he sees me, to get the . . ." She drew her eyebrows together, trying to find the right word. "To get the whole picture."

Rebecca pretended to think it over. "That's a good idea. You can wait in your room until he gets home, and when he's comfortable, I'll call upstairs and you can come down. How's that?"

Melinda hugged her, right there in the shopping mall, and when she did, people stopped and smiled. One woman said, "What a lovely picture the two of you make. Mother and daughter. How nice."

* * *

It was a little after five when Tom came in. Rebecca, who was in the living room, got up to greet him. He kissed her. "Did you have a nice day?" he asked.

"I had a wonderful day." She smiled. "Melinda and I went shopping."

"Where is she?"

"Upstairs. She's excited about her birthday tomorrow."

"I'd have liked to have had a party for her, but there just wasn't time to get things together. I thought that after church the three of us could go somewhere special for dinner."

They were going to church together.

Little warning bells went off in Rebecca's head. She took a steadying breath and suggested, "Why don't you sit down and let me fix you a drink, Tom? We have plenty of time before dinner." She went to the sideboard and began to make his drink. "How did it go at the college?"

"Good." He rubbed his hands together. "It was good to be back, Rebecca. School started last week, and one of the professors, Ross Contney, took over for me. I'll have a lot of catching up to do, but it's going to be all right."

Rebecca handed him his drink. "I told Melinda I'd let her know when you got home."

She started out of the room, but he took her hand to hold her back. "I'm glad the two of you are getting along," he said. "It means a lot to me that you are."

"She's a lovely little girl, Tom. You should be very proud of her."

"I am," he said. "And of you, too." He kissed her and let her go.

She went to the bottom of the stairs, and as they had planned, she called up, "Melinda. Your dad's home."

"Okay," Melinda answered in a nervous squeak. "I'll be right there." Then she whispered, "Wait for me, okay?"

"Okay," Rebecca whispered back.

Two minutes later she came down, smoothing the skirt of the blue velvet dress. "Do I look all right? Is my hair okay?"

"You look beautiful, Mellie."

"Do I really?" Still standing on the stairway, the little girl put her arms around Rebecca's neck and gave her a quick hug. Then, hand in hand, they went into the living room.

"There you are," Tom said. "I wondered where..." He stared at his child and at the woman who stood beside her, holding her hand. He was too moved for a moment even to speak.

"Becky bought me the dress for my birthday," Melinda said nervously. "And then we got my hair cut." She chewed on her bottom lip. "Do you like it, Dad? Do I look all right?"

"You look..." He swallowed hard. "You look beautiful."

She smiled up at Rebecca. Then letting go of her hand, she ran to her father and threw her arms around him.

He hugged her to him. "I love you, baby," he said against her hair. And over her shoulder he looked at Rebecca. "And you," he whispered. "And you."

Chapter 16

"Mine eyes have seen the glory…" sang the parishioners of the Brookfield Falls Community Church. Men and women wearing their Sunday best, restless children with apple-red cheeks, elderly ladies with beauty-shopped hair. Husbands and wives. Families.

For Rebecca there was a sense of unreality about all of it. It was as though she were playing a scene in one of her father's television productions, a variation of *Our Town*. Small-town America at its finest.

Breakfast with Tom and Melinda this morning had been like a Norman Rockwell painting. The three of them in the breakfast nook. Bright yellow tablecloth, yellow curtains at the window that overlooked the side garden. Mrs. Plum had been at the stove making waffles and frying sausage when someone knocked at the door.

"I'll answer that," Tom had said.

"I wonder who in the world it could be." Melinda had said, taking a sip of her orange juice. "Nobody ever comes to call on a Sunday morning."

There had been voices, the sound of the front door closing, and Tom had come back into the kitchen carrying a wicker basket with a red ribbon tied on the handle.

"Happy birthday, sprite," he'd said. But his voice had been almost drowned out by a plaintive whine as a soft brown and white nose, followed by moist brown eyes had poked over the top of the basket.

"A dog!" Melinda had squealed, and then the pup was in her arms, licking her face, and she had looked so little-girl happy that it was all Rebecca could do not to burst into tears.

Now here she was in church, sharing a hymnal with Melinda, singing "The Battle Hymn of the Republic" with the rest of the congregation. But not really part of them. Never a part of them.

After the service, people came up to Tom to shake his hand and clap a friendly hand on his shoulder. "Everybody was worried about you," they told him. "You've been away too long. We're glad you're back."

And the minister, Reverend Jonathan Dodd, said, "We've missed you, Tom. There hasn't been a day gone by when you weren't in our prayers."

The words were heartfelt and sincere. These people really cared about Tom, and they were concerned about what happened to him. There was warmth in their handclasps, true affection in their eyes. There was such a feeling of community here.

Rebecca smiled when Tom said, "This is Rebecca Bliss. She's going to be staying with us for a while."

Men and women shook hands with her. The minister asked, "Where are you from, Miss Bliss?"

"New York."

"I imagine you're finding life here in Brookfield Falls a little different than the city."

A lot different, she wanted to say. But instead, she said, "It's a charming town." And she meant it.

The minister looked down at Melinda. "My, don't you look pretty."

"It's my birthday," the little girl said.

"Congratulations," Reverend Dodd smiled. "Are you going to do something special today?"

"We're going to the fair over in Littlefield, and afterward we're going to the River Inn for dinner."

"Well, you folks have a real nice day," he said.

It was a real nice day. The fair turned out to be fun. There was a Ferris wheel and a carousel, stands of homemade preserves, chutney and chowchow, corn salad and pickle relish, applesauce cakes and rhubarb pies, bread and butter pickles, and cotton candy.

Melinda rode the carousel and the three of them went on the Ferris wheel. Tom won a fluffy pink elephant for Melinda and a round glass paperweight with a tiny old-fashioned sleigh and horses inside for Rebecca.

"It'll snow if you turn it upside down," Melinda said.

It was almost four by the time they left the fair and headed back to Brookfield Falls and the restaurant by the river. It was a pleasant drive, with Melinda in the back seat chattering away, Rebecca next to Tom in the front.

And again, for Rebecca, there was an overwhelming sense of unreality about all of it, as though any moment now she would awaken and find herself back in her New York apartment. But there were no skyscrapers here, no roar of traffic. Instead, the road they took was lined with sturdy white oaks, shagbark hickories, box elders and sugar maples, all alive with the changing colors of autumn. Instead of Saks and Bloomingdale's there were fields ready for the harvest. Instead of skyscrapers there were farmhouses, red barns and cattle grazing in the pastures.

She looked at Tom. As though memorizing every detail of his face, she studied the line of his brow, the strong nose, the mouth, the jut of the jaw. And his wonderfully sensitive hands. Because she couldn't help herself she placed her hand over his. He smiled at her, and when he did, something seemed to give way inside of her and she felt a rush of emotion that almost overwhelmed her. She wanted to be close to him, a part of him. She wanted all sorts of things she couldn't even give name to. But knew somehow that she could never have them.

They arrived at the inn at twilight. An old-fashioned yellow house with a porch all across the front, it was on the riverbank and was surrounded by willow trees. Inside there were soft lights and a big stone fireplace at the far end of the room. A middle-aged woman with a pleasant, friendly face and a starchy white apron over her dark blue dress greeted them. "Three for dinner?" she asked. "I have a nice table near the fire. Come right this way, folks."

Melinda and Rebecca preceded Tom, and as he watched them weave their way through the tables, he was filled with a sense of pride. People turned to look at them, and he knew they were thinking that they were mother and daughter. And with that thought came a longing greater than anything he had ever known that this could be true, that they could be a family. There was such a sense of rightness about their being together like this, and he hoped that Rebecca could see it as he did.

He thought then of the past five years since Beth's death, and he knew now how lonely he had been, how very much he had longed for someone to share his life with, someone who would love him, and Melinda. Someone like Rebecca.

When they reached the table and he seated her, his hands lingered for a moment on her shoulders and he gave them a gentle squeeze, a silent communication to try to tell her how happy he was that she was here. And that he loved her.

The dinner, roast duck for Tom and Rebecca, fried chicken for Melinda, was delicious. Touching his glass of apple cider to Rebecca's and then to Melinda's, he said, "Here's to the birthday girl."

"And to Becky." Melinda smiled at her. "I wish you could stay forever."

Tom touched his glass to Rebecca's. "So do I," he said.

She looked at him and at his daughter and she felt a sudden hunger, a longing, and yes, for the first time a sense of doubt about the life she lived and about the work she did. She thought about Caracas and about San Sebastian and all of the other times her life had been in jeopardy. She looked around this warm and pleasant room, and though she didn't want to, she couldn't help comparing her life to the life here in Brookfield Falls. She could easily... No! She gave herself a mental shake. No, she couldn't. She mustn't give in to this. It wasn't the kind of life she wanted.

Tom was wrong; she didn't belong here. She could never belong.

And suddenly, for a reason she couldn't explain, she was so overcome by sadness that it was all she could do not to burst into tears.

Like falling leaves, the days of autumn drifted by. A few days became a week, a few weeks became a month. Every day Rebecca told herself that it was time to leave, but she didn't go.

It's because I need this time to rest, she told herself. I'll tell Tom and I'll make a reservation to fly back to New York next week. But before she could tell him of her decision, Mrs. Plum's sister called from Chicago.

"She's real bad off, sir," Mrs. Plum told Tom. "I've got to go, at least for a week or two."

"Of course you do," he said. "We'll miss you, Mrs. Plum, but don't worry. We'll manage."

And suddenly, although Tom didn't ask her to, Rebecca found herself taking on the duties of running a house. It was a new experience for her, and one she was determined to cope with for as long as she was here.

Every morning she fixed breakfast for Tom and Melinda. Or tried to. She burned the bacon and the toast, undercooked the eggs and made the coffee too strong.

Melinda said, "I love crisp bacon," and Tom said that the coffee really got him going in the morning.

For dinner she tried to make a pot roast like Mrs. Plum's, but it came out of the oven burnt on the outside and undercooked on the inside. She tried meat loaf, but it tasted mealy. She fried chicken and managed to burn it, along with her finger.

Mollie, the collie pup, was eating well. The rest of them were going to bed hungry.

"I'm a total bust as a homemaker," Rebecca said the night after the fried chicken disaster.

"No, you're not." Tom kissed her burned finger.

"I'm the world's worst cook."

"Not the worst." He smiled. "But you're right up there with 'em."

She socked him on his shoulder, then leaned her head against his chest. "I'm not any good at this. I'm just not cut out for this kind of life. It's time I went back to New York." She looked up at him. "I'll leave as soon as Mrs. Plum comes back."

"No." He put a finger under her chin. "I don't want you to leave." And he lifted her face to his and kissed her.

He had meant it to be a light kiss, but that wasn't what it turned out to be. It was a kiss filled with all of the pent-up longing and desire too long held in check. His body was hard against hers, his passion barely controlled. And though Rebecca knew she should move away, that this was neither the time nor the place for an embrace, she answered his kiss with an intensity of emotion that left them both breathless.

"I'm so hungry for you," he whispered against her lips. "I want you, Rebecca. Lord, how I want you! It's been weeks since we've made love."

"Propriety." She sighed and stepped away from him. "One doesn't when one is around children."

"One does if one is married."

"Tom . . ."

"I love you, Rebecca. I want to marry you. I want to be able to go up the stairs with you every night for the rest of our lives. I want to sleep with you and make love with you. I want to wake up in the morning with you beside me. I want you. I want..." With a low groan of need Tom pulled her into his arms again. "Don't you know how much I love you?"

Rebecca had known that this was coming, but now that the moment was here she wasn't prepared for it.

"Tom," she said. "Tom, I—"

He stopped her words with a kiss so fierce with hunger and with need that it took away her breath. She leaned into him, holding him as he held her, seeking his mouth as he sought hers. He touched her breast, and she smothered her cry against his mouth. And knew that if she didn't stop, if she didn't step away very quickly, that they would make love. And that they shouldn't. For though she thought of herself as a modern woman who believed in sexual freedom, there was in her a sense of propriety and of concern for his child who might, for whatever reason, be aware of their making love.

She clung to him for a moment longer, then with a low cry she backed away and said, "We can't, Tom. I'm sorry, but we can't."

He looked at her, his eyes hooded, his nostrils flaring with desire.

She laid her hand on his chest. "Please," she said, and he let her go.

They stood there at the bottom of the stairs for a long moment before he said, "We have to talk about this, Rebecca."

"I know."

"Tomorrow?"

"Tom, I—"

"Meet me after school, along the river walk. We'll talk then." He took her hand that still rested against his chest. Then, bringing it up, he turned it and kissed her palm. "I love you. Remember that when you go to sleep tonight."

There was a hint of frost in the air when Rebecca left the house. She wore gray flannel pants, a matching cashmere sweater and wool tweed jacket that she had bought the week before in a boutique just off the main street. She had slept little the night before, and when she saw Tom for breakfast that morning, she'd known that he hadn't rested any better than she had.

They didn't have much to say to each other at breakfast; Melinda had done most of the talking. When it was time for her to leave for school, Rebecca had handed her her bright red lunch box and said, "I'm going to walk down to the river and meet your dad after school this afternoon. It'll probably be five or after before we get home."

"It'll be kind of late to start dinner then." Melinda looked hopeful. "Maybe we could eat out."

"That's a great idea." Rebecca had kissed her goodbye. "Have a good day," she said.

Now, as she made her way down toward the river walk, she thought how accustomed she had become to sitting at the breakfast table every morning with Tom and Melinda. And of how she would miss them when she left.

Her fingers curled inside the pockets of her jacket. It was going to be hard, so hard to tell Tom of her decision.

She left the sidewalk and went through the trees to the cobbled path that bordered the river. It was so lovely here this time of the year, and she wondered what it would look like in the winter when the grass and the trees were covered with snow, and in the spring when everything came to life again. She wondered, but she wouldn't be here to see it.

Tom saw her before she saw him, and he smiled because he liked the way she walked with her shoulders back, her arms swinging free. And he thought how natural she looked in this setting. Can't she see it? he asked himself. Doesn't she understand how well she fits in here? How right this would be for her? He thought of the danger of her job, and knew that if she went back, there wasn't any way he could be with her to protect her. I won't let her go, he told himself. I won't let her go back to it.

She saw him watching her, waved and hurried toward him. "Isn't this the most gorgeous day?" she said in a rush of words. "Don't you just love this time of year? It's lovely in New York now, too. Did you know that? The flower shops along Madison Avenue are filled with fall flowers—chrysanthemums, jack-o'-lanterns and pussy willows. And the store windows are decorated..." She stopped and laughed nervously. "I love this time of the year."

"Yes, so do I. But this is where I want to be when fall comes, Rebecca. I want to be here." He took her hands. "With you."

"Tom—"

"Let's walk," he said abruptly as he reached for her hand and headed down the river path. There was a chill in the air, and because of the chill and the hour there was no one else around. It was very quiet, with only the small slap of the water against the shore and the rustle of dry leaves underfoot.

They walked for a long time without speaking, and when they came to a bench, Tom said, "Let's sit down, Rebecca."

She gazed at the scene around her, moved by the quiet beauty, and said, "It's lovely here, Tom. I'm so glad I came."

"Then why do you want to leave?"

"I have a job."

"I hate what you do."

"I know." She reached for his hand. "But I'm good at what I do, Tom. And somebody has to do it."

"But not you," he said.

"It won't be forever."

"How long have you been in the organization?"

"Five years."

"You've had two close calls, at least that I know of. How many more were there, Rebecca? How long before . . . ?" He had to steel himself to say the words. "How long before your luck runs out?"

Her expression grew serious. "I'm going to quit. In a few years—"

"A few years? One or two? Three?" He shook his head. "I love you, Rebecca. And I need you. I need you now."

She tried to find the words that would make him understand. "I love you, too," she said at last. "You know I do. It won't be goodbye when I leave. You and Melinda mean so much to me, Tom. We'll stay in touch. You can come to New York—"

"When you're between assignments?" He shook his head. "No," he said. "I don't want a long-distance relationship, Rebecca. I want us to be a family now, not three or four years from now."

He stood, hands in his pockets and looked out at the river. The afternoon had faded into evening. A cold wind whispered through the trees. Low clouds gathered and the smell of rain was in the air. The river that only a little while ago had seemed so calm had turned gray and choppy. "I need you," he said. "I need you to be waiting for me when I come home at night. I have love and warmth to give, Rebecca. I want to give them to you."

"Tom, darling . . ." Her eyes filled.

"I've been alone too long, Rebecca." There was a great sadness in his voice, and a firmness she had never heard before. "I won't wait another two or three years. I can't."

She swallowed hard. "Are you saying . . . ?"

"I want someone to share my life with." A muscle jumped in his cheek. "I'm afraid that if it isn't you . . ." His eyes were bleak. "I need you so."

She felt cold, and knew that the coldness wasn't from the chill in the air but from a chill that came from deep within her. Tom wasn't threatening; he was simply stating the truth. He *did* need someone, and so did Melinda.

"I need time," she said. "Please, Tom. Please give me a little more time. I want to be the woman you want me to be, but I've gotten so used to the way I live . . ." She swallowed hard. "It's difficult."

He put his arms around her. "You're going to have to make a decision."

"Will you give me a little more time? A week? A month?"

"If you'll stay here. Until you decide, I mean."

"Yes, Tom. Until I decide."

He leaned his face against hers and they stood there, holding each other. Then finally, arm in arm, they went back up the path and started home.

"There was a phone call for you, Becky," Melinda said as soon as they came in the door. "From Washington, D.C. From a man named—" Melinda looked at the paper in her hand "—Mr. Hayden. He sounded real grouchy."

Alex. Rebecca took a deep breath. "I have to call him," she told Tom.

She felt him stiffen. "Of course. Use the phone in the den." He didn't look at her. He put his arm around Melinda's shoulders. "How about a pizza tonight?"

Rebecca stood for a moment, then she went into the den and closed the door.

"It's Rebecca," she said when Alex answered.

"How're you feeling?"

"I'm all right."

"I need you back here, Becky. ASAP!"

"Alex, I—"

"It's Caracas again."

"Can't you…?" She wet her lips. "Can't you send someone else?"

"You know the setup there. You're the one for the job. It'll take a couple of weeks to get the operation organized, but I need you right away so that you and Ed can arrange the contacts. You're booked on a flight out of Chicago tomorrow morning. I'll have somebody meet you at this end."

"I'd planned on staying here a little while longer."

"Plans change." Hayden cleared his throat. "How are things going between you and the professor?"

"All right."

"Had enough of Hooterville?"

She tightened her hand around the receiver.

"Be good for you to get back into action, Becky. I'll see you tomorrow."

"Alex, I—"

"Tomorrow," he said.

Rebecca put the receiver down. Caracas, she thought. Oh, God, not Caracas. And not tomorrow. It was too soon. She couldn't... She took a deep, shaking breath. She had to tell Tom. And Melinda. She didn't have any choice. This was her job. She had to go.

She opened the door and went out just as Melinda came bounding down the stairs. "We're going out for pizza," the little girl said. "Hurry up, Becky. Get your coat."

Rebecca forced a smile, but the smile faltered when she saw Tom. "I... I talked to Alex."

He waited.

She cleared her throat. "I have to leave."

"When?"

"Tomorrow."

"I see."

"You're gonna leave?" Melinda looked at her, unbelieving. "Why, Becky? Why?"

"I have to go back to work, honey."

"But I thought you were going to stay with us. I thought—"

"Go back upstairs and get your coat, Mellie," Tom said.

"But—"

"Go on." And when she did, he looked at Rebecca. "You don't have to go."

"Yes, I do."

"I see." He pinched the skin between his eyebrows. "Another assignment?"

She nodded. "Caracas."

"Caracas?"

"I know the situation there. I'm the right one for the job." She looked up at him. "After that—"

"After that there'll be another job, and another."

"No, I—"

"Yes, there will." He shook his head, then turned away. "You'd better take a coat. It's going to be cold tonight."

Chapter 17

Mrs. Plum had returned and things were back to the way they had been before Rebecca had come into their lives. But because she had come into their lives everything was different.

He hadn't realized how difficult it would be without her.

Melinda was quieter. She moped about the house, and sometimes, when she didn't realize he was watching her, there was an expression on her face that he had never seen before, a strangely bereft look that made him want to gather her into his arms. She spent a lot of time in her room or in front of the television set in the den, a worried expression in her bright blue eyes. Mollie would always be beside Melinda, her head on the little girl's lap.

He wanted to say, "Mollie's not supposed to be up on the furniture," but he didn't because he knew that his daughter needed whatever comfort the collie had to give.

As for himself, he went through the days after Rebecca's departure in a kind of daze. They had had little to say to each other the morning he had driven her to the airport in Chicago. He had put her luggage on the sidewalk and motioned to a skycap.

"I won't come in," he'd said. "I have to get back for a ten o'clock class."

"Of course." She looked at him, then away. "I'll call you tonight from Washington."

"Fine."

"Thank you..." she said. "I'm very grateful... Tell Melinda..."

He heard the tremble in her voice. "I'm sorry, Tom," she whispered.

"Yes," he said. "So am I."

"I love you."

She waited for him to say, I love you, too, but instead he only said, "I know."

"I have to go now, darling."

Darling. That almost undid him. "You'd better hurry," he told her.

She turned away. He said, "Rebecca?" And suddenly she was in his arms and she was crying and saying, "Tom. Oh, Tom." Then she had stepped away from him, and before he could stop her she had run into the terminal.

He couldn't sleep. Each night after he kissed Melinda good-night and tucked her into bed, he came back downstairs, turned the television on, sat in front of it and watched the screen with unseeing eyes, willing the time to pass and sleep to come.

One night, very late, Melinda had come downstairs, Mollie trailing behind her. "Daddy," she'd said. "You fell asleep, Daddy."

She rarely called him that, and because she did he had known that she'd done it out of a need to feel close and loved. He'd taken her up on his lap and hugged and kissed her, and when she fell asleep, he'd carried her back up to her bed.

After that he tried to pretend that everything was as it had once been. He made himself eat breakfast with her and he tried to do all the things she liked to do, even if it meant eating pizza five times a week.

"Becky likes anchovies and olives on her pizza," Melinda said. "Isn't that funny? She watches real gushy love stories on television and she cries and says, 'Isn't that wonderful?'"

And sometimes Melinda said, "I miss her, Daddy. Why did she leave? Was it because of me? Did I do something bad?"

"No, Mellie," Tom always answered. "Of course you didn't do anything bad. Becky loves you, sweetheart. She wanted to stay with us, but she has a job she had to get back to."

"Why?"

"It's what she does, Mellie."

"But she could marry you then she wouldn't have to work." She frowned at him. "How come you let her go, Dad? How come you didn't ask her to marry you?"

Not sure that he should, he said, "I did, Mellie. But Becky has her own life. I guess she just isn't ready to settle down."

A week passed. Two weeks. He moved like an automaton, feeling as though he were locked somewhere between past and present. He tried, for Melinda's sake, to pretend that everything was as it had once been. But it wasn't; nothing would ever be the same again.

He kissed Melinda goodbye every morning. He taught his classes and did all the things he had done before Rebecca had come into his life. And sometimes on the way back from the college in the late afternoon he walked down by the river where they had walked. The trees were almost bare of leaves now and the wind off the river was cold, a portent of the winter to come.

She had been gone almost three weeks when the phone call came.

"I just wanted to say hello," she said when Tom answered. "I'll be out of touch for a while. I wanted you to know."

"When are you leaving?"

"On Friday. How... how are you, Tom?"

"Fine, thank you."

"And Melinda?"

"She's right here. Would you like to say hello?"

"Yes, please."

"It's Becky," he said. "She wants to talk to you."

"Really?" Her eyes lit up. "Hi," she said. "Hi, Becky. We really miss you. When are you coming back?"

Tom walked over to the fireplace. He poked at a fallen log so that he wouldn't hear Melinda's end of the conversation. She talked for ten minutes, her voice bubbling with excitement until he heard her say, "But why can't you? Daddy and I miss you so much, Becky. Why do you have to go away? When you come back from your trip, will you come see us?" And finally she said goodbye and handed the receiver to him.

He said hello again, but it was a moment before Rebecca answered. And when she did, he knew that she was crying.

"I'll call when I come back," she said at last.

"I don't suppose you have any idea when that will be."

"No, I . . . I don't."

"Well . . ." Tom cleared his throat. "Take care of yourself."

"Of course."

"Goodbye, Rebecca."

"Bye, Tom."

He heard the click on the other end of the phone, and still he stood there, holding the receiver against his ear. "Becky," he whispered into the now-dead phone. "Becky."

She thought of the Sunday they had gone to the fair, and when she closed her eyes, it seemed to her that she could hear the music of the carousel. And see Melinda, the fair hair tossed back from her shoulders, clinging to the mane of the black horse that went round and round, laughing down at them, saying, "This is the best day ever."

Rebecca picked up the paperweight that Tom had won for her.

"It'll snow if you turn it upside down," Melinda had said.

She turned it upside down and watched the silvery white flakes drift down on the old-fashioned sleigh and the tiny horses. And she remembered that after the fair, when they went to the inn for dinner, how

Tom's hands had lingered on her shoulders when he seated her.

And suddenly, as Rebecca held the paperweight in her hands, she remembered her mother's words the first time she had ever seen her. "I didn't know. I just didn't know," her mother had whispered. "We make choices in our lives, Becky. I thought I made the right choice, but I was wrong." And there had been an expression on her mother's face, an expression of such pain, such anguish, an expression Rebecca had never forgotten.

She turned the paperweight over and watched the flakes drift gently down. And it seemed to her that she could see Melinda among the tiny figures, and hear her child's voice saying, "Why do you have to go away, Becky? Why?"

And Tom's voice whispering, "I love you, Rebecca. I want us to be a family…"

"I won't wait for another two or three years," he had said. "I can't."

"Tom," she whispered. "Oh, Tom."

The telephone jangled. She picked up the receiver and said in an unsteady voice, "Yes?"

"You all set?" Alex asked.

She took a deep breath. "Yes, all set."

"I've got a car waiting downstairs. Plane leaves in an hour."

"I'm ready."

"Stop into my office before you leave."

"Right." She hung up, and when she realized she was still holding the paperweight, she put it down with a smothered sigh and picked up her purse and the one suitcase she would carry. She went down the corridor to Alex's office and went in.

"Need anything?" he asked.

She shook her head.

"Gonzales will meet your plane."

"Okay."

"This isn't going to be anything like the other time. Everything got fouled up then. You'll be better protected now."

"Sure," Rebecca said. "It'll be a piece of cake."

He looked at her, frowning. "I wouldn't send you if I didn't have to."

"That's what you say every time."

"You're the best I've got."

"You say that, too."

"Damn it, Becky, what's the matter with you? What—?"

A door in the outer office slammed. Then another one. Somebody called out, "You can't come in here!"

Somebody else said, "The hell I can't!"

Alex shoved his chair back. "What's going on out there?" he shouted.

A secretary opened the door. "Sir, there's a man here demanding to see Miss Bliss. I tried to stop him, but he—"

Tom stepped around her. "Where is she?" he roared. "Where...?" He saw Rebecca. "Thank God," he said. "I was afraid I'd missed you."

"Tom? What...?" She stared at him. "What are you doing here?"

"I've come to take you home."

"But I—"

"Who in the hell do you think you are, busting in like this?" Alex barreled around his desk, his face red with anger and outrage. "You've no business being here, Thornton, so get the hell out."

"Not without Rebecca." Fists clenched at his sides, Tom glared at the other man.

"She works for me."

"Not anymore."

"Tom, I—"

"Is that your suitcase, Rebecca?"

"Yes, but—"

He picked it up. "Come on."

"I . . . I can't. There's a car waiting. I have to catch a plane. I have to go to Caracas."

He put the suitcase down. "The only thing you have to do is marry me." Ignoring Alex Hayden, he stepped closer to Rebecca and put his hands on her shoulders. "I love you. I care about you." He looked beyond her to Hayden, and his arms tightened on her shoulders. "You're not going to work for him anymore, Rebecca. You're leaving with me now."

"Darling, I—"

He stopped her words with a hard, angry kiss, and when he let her go, he picked up the suitcase again. "Come on."

Rebecca looked at him, almost too dazed to speak. But Alex spoke. He shouted, "Now see here—"

"Melinda's waiting for us downstairs," Tom said. "Are you coming?"

She looked at him, then she looked at Alex, and at the startled secretary, and past the secretary to where Ed Blakley stood, smiling and giving her a thumbs-up signal. She took a deep breath. "Wait here," she said to Tom.

She went back to her office and picked up the glass paperweight. She turned it upside down again, and now it seemed to her as though she could see three tiny figures—her own and Tom's and Melinda's. She clutched it to her breast and went out of her office without looking back.

"I didn't want to leave without this," she said when she went back to the office where Tom waited.

The tension went out of his face. "Are you ready now?"

"Yes, darling. I'm ready."

Hayden put a restraining hand on her arm. "You can't do this."

"Yes, I can." She smiled gently. "I'm sorry, Alex. But you're wrong, you know. There really is someone else. There's always someone else." She reached for Tom's hand. "Let's go home."

Epilogue

The snow began to fall on Christmas Eve. It fell all that night, and by Christmas morning the town of Brookfield Falls was knee-deep in drifts.

"It looks like your paperweight," Melinda said from her chair by the fireplace. She reached down to pet the ever-faithful Mollie. "It's so pretty I hope it snows forever."

"No, you don't." Tom smiled at her. "If it kept snowing, you wouldn't be able to go back to school next week."

"That's what I mean," she answered with a grin.

Rebecca leaned her head against Tom's arm. It was going to be a lovely Christmas, the best Christmas she had ever had. Earlier this week she and Melinda had decorated the inside of the house with bright red ribbons and bows, Christmas candles, holly and mistletoe. Tom had bought a tree that was as tall as he was, and that night the three of them had sat in front of the

fireplace stringing popcorn and cranberries to deco-
rate the tree, because, Melinda had said, it was something she had always wanted to do.

It was a beautiful tree, sparkling with lights, laden
with silvery tinsel and Christmas balls, some of them
new, some of them saved from when Tom was a boy.

Only three months had gone by since that day Tom
had stormed into the Washington office of SIS, demanding that she leave with him, but it seemed as
though she had always been here.

They had been married a week after they returned
to Brookfield Falls. The wedding had taken place at
the Brookfield Community Church. The church so-
loist had sung "Oh Perfect Love," and the Reverend
Jonathan Dodd had performed the ceremony. Melinda, who had acted as Rebecca's maid of honor, had
worn her blue velvet dress. Rebecca had worn white.
She and Tom had spent a weekend honeymoon at a
small resort hotel on the river near Brookfield Falls.
They'd taken long walks in the crisp fall air, they'd
talked of how their life together would be, and they
had made love. Sweet, deep, hungry love.

"It will always be like this," he'd said.

"Yes," she'd answered. "Always." And she had
known in her heart that it was true.

She felt no regrets at having left the life she had
known or her job with SIS, for somehow she had
known that Tom was right. She'd had one too many
narrow escapes, and the time had come to lower the
curtain on that part of her life.

This morning she had telephoned her father to wish
him a Merry Christmas. He'd been glad to hear from
her, but he couldn't talk too long, he'd said, because
he was on his way to a cocktail brunch at Pavillon.

When she put the receiver down, she had felt a twinge of sadness because things hadn't changed between them. But it was all right; she had her own family now. She belonged.

A choir of voices sang "Adeste Fideles" on the stereo. Wonderful smells drifted in from the kitchen where Mrs. Plum had been busy since early this morning. Tom's housekeeper had planned to start the dinner and then to take a bus to Chicago to spend the day with her sister. Now, because of the snow, she would have Christmas dinner with them.

Several times Rebecca had gone to the kitchen and offered to help. But Mrs. Plum had shooed her out, saying, "No, no, dearie. You go back with your husband and your daughter."

Her husband and her daughter. She squeezed Tom's hand, and when he turned to smile at her, she said, "Thank you, Tom."

"For what, sweetheart?"

"For everything. For coming to Washington after me. For this house, for Christmas, for Melinda." She squeezed his hand. "For your love."

He kissed her. "I love you so much."

"And I love you, Tom."

In a little while Mrs. Plum came in to announce that dinner was ready. "You two sit down," she told Rebecca and Tom. "Melinda and I will bring everything in."

Candles were lighted. The roast turkey, browned crisp and golden, was placed before Tom for carving. Melinda brought in the mashed potatoes and sweet potatoes. There was cranberry sauce, vegetables, a Waldorf salad and hot, flaky biscuits.

When they were all seated, Tom poured wine for the three of them, apple cider for Melinda.

"I'll have apple cider, too," Rebecca said.

"You don't want any wine?"

"No, thank you, Tom. I really prefer the cider."

He raised an eyebrow, but didn't question her. "Well," he said. "I guess we're ready. Melinda, will you say grace?"

They joined hands, and for once Melinda didn't race through the prayer, but spoke slowly, sweetly, giving a deeper meaning to the old, familiar words. And she added, "God bless Dad and Becky and Mrs. Plum. And thank you for letting Dad bring Becky back home to us."

"That was very nice, sprite," Tom said. "Thank you." He picked up the carving knife. "Shall we begin?"

"Not quite yet," Rebecca said.

They looked at her. Mrs. Plum asked, "What is it, dearie? Aren't you feeling well?"

"I'm feeling very well, Mrs. Plum. Thank you." She looked at Tom and Melinda. "I have some news. This seemed like a good time to tell you about it."

Tom reached for her hand. Just for a moment she saw his eyes darken, and because she knew that he was afraid she might be going to tell him she was going back, she said, "It's good news. I think you'll be pleased."

"What? What is it?" Melinda leaned forward. "What is it, Becky?"

"We're going to have a baby," Rebecca said.

"A baby?" Melinda clapped her hands. "We're going to have a baby!"

And Mrs. Plum said, "Now isn't that the nicest Christmas present ever?"

"Rebecca . . . ?" Tom looked dumbstruck. "Are . . . are you sure?"

"Very sure, darling. Are you pleased?"

"Pleased!" He pushed his chair back, then hers, and brought her up into his arms. "It's wonderful news, Rebecca. Wonderful! Are you all right? Is everything—"

"Everything's fine," she said with a laugh. "Are you happy, Tom?"

"Happy?" Tears stung his eyes, but he wasn't ashamed of them because they were happy tears. He kissed Rebecca again, and with his arms still around her he gazed around the table. "Merry Christmas," he said. "Merry Christmas, everybody."

*   *   *   *   *

INTIMATE MOMENTS®
™ Silhouette

Ever since the appearance of Linda Howard's incredibly popular MACKENZIE'S MOUNTAIN in 1989, we've received literally hundreds of letters, all asking that same question. At last the book we've all been waiting for is here.

In September, look for MACKENZIE'S MISSION (Intimate Moments #445), Joe's story as only Linda Howard could tell it.

And Joe is only the first of an exciting breed here at Silhouette Intimate Moments. Starting in September, we'll be bringing you one title every month in our new **American Heroes** program. In addition to Linda Howard, the **American Heroes** lineup will be written by such stars as Kathleen Eagle, Kathleen Korbel, Patricia Gardner Evans, Marilyn Pappano, Heather Graham Pozzessere and more. Don't miss a single one!

It's Opening Night in October—
and you're invited!
Take a look at romance with a
brand-new twist, as the stars
of tomorrow make their
debut today!
It's LOVE:
an age-old story—
now, with
*WORLD PREMIERE
APPEARANCES* by:

Patricia Thayer—Silhouette Romance #895
JUST MAGGIE—Meet the Texas rancher who wins this pretty
teacher's heart...and lose your own heart, too!

Anne Marie Winston—Silhouette Desire #742
BEST KEPT SECRETS—Join old lovers reunited and see what
secret wonders have been hiding...beneath the flames!

Sierra Rydell—Silhouette Special Edition #772
ON MIDDLE GROUND—Drift toward Twilight, Alaska, with this
widowed mother and collide—heart first—into body heat
enough to melt the frozen tundra!

Kate Carlton—Silhouette Intimate Moments #454
KIDNAPPED!—Dare to look on as a timid wallflower blos-
soms and falls in fearless love—with her gruff, mysterious
kidnapper!

Don't miss the classics of tomorrow—
premiering today—only from

PREM

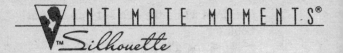

**Welcome to Conard County, Wyoming, where the
sky spreads bold and blue above men and women
who draw their strength from the wild western land
and from the bonds of the love they share.**

Join author Rachel Lee for a trip to the American West
as we all want it to be. In Conard County, Wyoming,
she's created a special place where men are men
and women are more than a match for them.

In the first book of the miniseries, EXILE'S END (Intimate
Moments #449), you'll meet Amanda Grant, whose
imagination takes her to worlds of wizards and
warlocks in the books she writes, but whose everyday
life is gray and forlorn—until Ransom Laird walks onto
her land with trouble in his wake and a promise in his
heart. Once you meet them, you won't want to stop
reading. And once you've finished the book, you'll be
looking forward to all the others in the miniseries,
starting with CHEROKEE THUNDER, available in
December.

EXILE'S END is available this September, only from
Silhouette Intimate Moments.

Take 4 bestselling love stories FREE

Plus get a FREE surprise gift!

Special Limited-time Offer

Mail to Silhouette Reader Service™

In the U.S.	In Canada
3010 Walden Avenue	P.O. Box 609
P.O. Box 1867	Fort Erie, Ontario
Buffalo, N.Y. 14269-1867	L2A 5X3

YES! Please send me 4 free Silhouette Intimate Moments® novels and my free surprise gift. Then send me 6 brand-new novels every month, which I will receive months before they appear in bookstores. Bill me at the low price of $2.96* each— a savings of 43¢ apiece off the cover prices. There are no shipping, handling or other hidden costs. I understand that accepting the books and gift places me under no obligation ever to buy any books. I can always return a shipment and cancel at any time. Even if I never buy another book from Silhouette, the 4 free books and the surprise gift are mine to keep forever.

*Offer slightly different in Canada—$2.96 per book plus 69¢ per shipment for delivery. Canadian residents add applicable federal and provincial sales tax. Sales tax applicable in N.Y.

245 BPA AGNP   345 BPA AGNQ

Name _____ (PLEASE PRINT)

Address _____ Apt. No. _____

City _____ State/Prov. _____ Zip/Postal Code. _____

This offer is limited to one order per household and not valid to present Silhouette Intimate Moments® subscribers. Terms and prices are subject to change.

MOM-92R   © 1990 Harlequin Enterprises Limited

TAKE A WALK ON THE DARK SIDE OF LOVE

October is the shivery season, when chill winds blow and shadows walk the night. Come along with us into a haunting world where love and danger go hand in hand, where passions will thrill you and dangers will chill you. Come with us to

In this newest short story collection from Silhouette Books, three of your favorite authors tell tales just perfect for a spooky autumn night. Let Anne Stuart introduce you to "The Monster in the Closet," Helen R. Myers bewitch you with "Seawitch," and Heather Graham Pozzessere entice you with "Wilde Imaginings."

Silhouette Shadows™
Haunting a store near you this October.

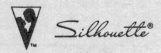